This book
belongs to

John. H. Boeing

contents

A DAILY EXPRESS PUBLICATION

© Beaverbrook Newspapers Ltd., 1975
Printed in Great Britain

80p

40p

RUPERT

After discovering that wonderful things can happen to anyone who drinks the water, Rupert does a good turn by giving Gaffer Jarge a few sips. But there is something that must be put right at once, as Rupert learns on meeting the busy little Imps of Spring.

RUPERT PROMISES TO TRY

"Some pussy-willow would look fine,"
Says Mummy, "in this vase of mine."

Smiles Rupert, "I will search for some,
Here's Bill! Perhaps he'd like to come."

ONE bright morning, while Rupert is in the garden, Mrs. Bear calls to him from the open window. "Yes, Mummy?" says Rupert. "Do you want me to run some errands?" Mrs. Bear shakes her head and shows him a large vase. "Spring is nearly here," she says, "and I'm trying to smarten up the cottage and make it look pretty. We have plenty of snowdrops and some crocuses, but they are all small, and I want some-thing to fill this big pot. D'you think you could find me some pussy-willow?" "I'll try," says Rupert. "I can hear Bill Badger at the gate. I'll get him to help me. Hi, Bill, we've got a job." The little badger waits to hear what Rupert wants. Then he chuckles. "Pussy-willow?" he grins. "Good gracious, Rupert, that's going to be quite difficult. I can't even remember what pussy-willow looks like. Anyway, I'll come with you."

and the
LITTLE RIVER

RUPERT AND BILL SET OUT

Across the countryside they trot,
"Hello, what's Simple Simon got?"

"I found this reed, with other ones,
Just where a tiny river runs."

Leaving the cottage Rupert and Bill trot across open country and past woods and bushes. "You'll have to tell me when you see some pussy-willow," says Bill, "otherwise I might pick something else by mistake." Although lots of little trees seem to be breaking into leaf, there is no sign of what they are seeking. "Perhaps it's too early in the season," says Bill. "How much farther do you want to search? Hello, there's

Simple Simon. He's carrying something. I wonder if that's pussy-willow he's found." As their pal approaches Rupert goes forward. "No, that's not pussy-willow," he says. "What is it? Where did you find it, Simon?" "I found it by a tiny river," says Simple Simon. "It must be a sort of reed, but I've never seen anything like it, though I know lots of wild plants. Just you feel it, Rupert. You'll be surprised."

RUPERT NOTICES A FROG

"It's light as dandelion's down!"
Says Rupert, with a puzzled frown.

"That's where the tiny river flows,"
Says Simon, and away he goes.

"It's just a little trickling rill,
It flows into that crack," says Bill.

"Whew!" Rupert gasps. "Did that frog fly?
How ever could it leap so high?"

Simple Simon hands over one of his big reeds. "It's pretty, isn't it?" he says, "but you feel how heavy it is." "Why, it has no weight at all," says Rupert. "It's just like holding nothing." "I'd like to pick some of this," says Bill. "I wonder if there's a mystery here." "Well, there's not much of it," says Simon, and pointing to a hillside he says that the little river is up there. Then they separate and, feeling still more mystified, Rupert and Bill set off. "Simon said the little river was on the hillside," murmurs Rupert as they begin to climb. "Surely rivers are generally at the bottom of the hills." "Look, there are some of those reeds!" calls Bill. "Perhaps it's up there." And, sure enough, just by the reeds there is a biggish trickle of water disappearing into a crack in the rock. As they move towards bigger plants higher up, something leaps away and disappears. "Whew! Did you see that?" gasps Rupert. "That was a frog, but it's no ordinary frog!"

6

RUPERT PICKS TWO REEDS

He stops to pick some nice tall reeds,
"They're just the thing my Mummy needs."

" It has no weight! It floats like fluff!
Here's a mystery, sure enough!"

Another frog leaps overhead,
It does not fall, but floats instead.

" I've found a pool! Quick, come and look!
It flows into our tiny brook."

"I'm sure this isn't pussy-willow," says Rupert, "but it should stand up well in that big pot at home and look nice. You'd better have some too and see if your Mummy knows what it is." Going to a higher clump he picks a fine stalk and hands it to Bill. Then he chooses another for himself. "I say, this one is lighter than ever," he mutters. "Look, when I let go it is hardly heavy enough to reach the ground. It's quite a mystery." While the two pals are puzzling over the light plants another frog suddenly leaps out from the reeds, right over their heads. "These plants aren't the only mystery here," exclaims Bill. "Who ever heard of a frog that could do that? It didn't seem to fall, it just floated down." "Let's try and see where it came from," says Rupert. Pushing up the slope he comes across a small, round pool. "Come and look at this," he calls. "There's water flowing out of it all the time but nothing seems to be flowing in. How strange!"

RUPERT ALSO TASTES A DROP

"A spring! It does look fresh and cool!"
Bill drinks some water from the pool.

Bill's scarcely swallowed half an ounce,
When all at once he starts to bounce!

"He can't stop jumping since that drink!
I'll try this water too, I think."

The chums now float and gently drop,
And neither knows just how to stop!

Rupert and Bill gaze at the quiet little pool with the trickle flowing out of it. "This must be what's called a spring," says Bill. "Do you suppose that this is the beginning of our little river? If it starts here and finishes at that little crack down below it must be the littlest river ever! It looks lovely water. I'd like to drink some." He does so, and almost at once begins to jerk up and down strangely. "Hi, d'you know what you're up to?" cries Rupert. "You're doing kneeling jumps!"

Bill tries to keep still. "I can't stop!" he gasps. "It's that water. Whenever I move I have to jump!" He tries to take a step and finds himself leaping right away from the pool. "I must try this," says Rupert, following him and taking a little drink from lower down the tiny river. Next minute both the pals are floating up and down, taking off whenever they try to walk and dropping gently back to earth. Up-down, up-down they go. In their surprise they can hardly find words to say.

RUPERT IS AS LIGHT AS AIR

"We're like these reeds, we have no weight!"
Says Bill. "We must investigate."

"I'll come back," Rupert Bear decides,
He bounds home with enormous strides.

Over the garden gate he soars,
And hops to Daddy, out of doors.

"My feet will hardly touch the ground!
I'm weightless! So's this plant I've found!"

At length both Rupert and Bill get more used to the problem of keeping themselves on the ground. "I feel just like these reeds, no weight at all," says Bill. "I suppose it must somehow be something strange in that river, though it all seems impossible. We must find some way of explaining it." "Right-ho, but first I must tell Mummy about it and ask if more of these plants will do instead of pussy-willow," says Rupert. So they go their separate ways, each stride taking them many yards.

Arriving near the cottage, Rupert finds it easy to take a little leap and send himself soaring over the gate, and then he hops round to where his Daddy is working. "Hello, Rupert! You seem very active. What are you bobbing about like that for?" says Mr. Bear. "Can't help it!" laughs Rupert. "I've hardly touched the ground all the way home, and it's hard to keep on it now. I've hardly got any weight. Nor has this plant that I've brought for Mummy. She wanted pussy-willow."

9

RUPERT LEAPS ON TO A ROOF

"That's pretty, with a nice long stem,"
Smiles Mummy. "I'd like more of them."

"My word, it's light, and feather soft!"
She gasps. "That leaf just stays aloft."

"We drank some water from a spring,
Now we can jump like anything!"

"I know that spring!" cries Mr. Bear.
"It's just plain water! Do take care!"

Hearing voices, Mummy comes out and learns something of Rupert's strange story. "I wish you'd try to keep still while you're talking," she says. "That branch you've brought isn't pussy-willow, but it's very pretty. I'd like some more. My, you said it was light, and it certainly is!" She picks a leaf and it floats for quite a time before settling very slowly on the grass. "I've never seen anything like it," says the mystified Mrs. Bear. "It's really a very strange plant. I wonder if it will ever wither." Daddy wants to hear more of Rupert's adventure. "Well, Simple Simon sent us to the clump of these big reeds," says Rupert, "and we found they only grew near a tiny river a few yards long, from a spring to a crack in the rock. Then Bill and I drank a little of the spring water, and now we can jump like anything. Look!" He gives a leap, and next moment he is right on top of the shed. "B-but I *know* that place!" gasps Mr. Bear. "It has always had ordinary cold water in it!"

RUPERT BORROWS A SMALL JUG

"Don't jump!" cries Mummy, all alert,
"Wait till we catch you! You'll get hurt!"

"I'll fetch some water, that is best,
Daddy shall put it to the test!"

"You'm lookin' sprightly!" Gaffer cries.
"Wish I was young again," he sighs.

Thinks Rupert, "My, how glad he'd be,
If he felt light, like Bill and me!"

Just as Rupert is poising himself to jump down from the shed, Mrs. Bear rushes forward. "Wait, wait till we catch you," she calls. "You'll hurt yourself on the stony path." "I'm all right!" smiles Rupert. "I don't feel heavy enough to hit anything hard." And he comes down quite gently. Later, indoors, when Mrs. Bear has got over her fright, he asks if he may go back. "Daddy knows that little spring, but he doesn't know the water that's in it now," he says. "May I fetch some in this small jug?" As Rupert is dancing back towards the spring he spies his old friend Gaffer Jarge. "Hi, young Rupert," wheezes the old man. "You'm lookin' happy. Where be gooin', jiggin' about like Jack-in-the-box? I wish I was your age!" Rupert waves a cheery greeting and leaps away to the clump of reeds that looks bigger than ever. "Poor old man," he thinks, glancing over his shoulder. "He does have to hobble slowly. How happy he would be if only he could feel as light as I do now!"

RUPERT GIVES GAFFER A SIP

He fills his small jug to the brim,
Then soars across the hedge to him.

" Try this!" He tells what has occurred,
" Then you'll feel light as any bird!"

As Gaffer drinks, a change takes place,
A dreamy smile lights up his face.

" I feel as light as any boy!
Tis magic!" And he jumps for joy.

Rupert decides to act on his kindly thought, and he fills the small jug with spring water before returning and suddenly rejoining Gaffer Jarge by soaring over a hedge. "Sakes alive, young Rupert! What be doin' up there?" croaks the aged man. Rupert smiles. "I thought you'd like to try jumping too, so I've brought you this," he says. And he tells the story of the spring. "Tchah, you and your tricks!" Gaffer frowns. "Know'd that spring all me life I have. Tis just plain water, no different from any other." Rupert insists that his story is true. "The plants up there are wonderful," he says. At length, still grumbling, Gaffer Jarge puts the jug to his lips. Gradually his expression changes. "You'm right! he whispers. "There's less weight already on me poor old legs." "That's fine, now try to jump," says Rupert. "Eh, I dursn't," says Gaffer, "not at my age." But he does try, and to his astonishment both his feet leave the grass together, and he jumps up and down.

RUPERT LOOKS ON ANXIOUSLY

The old man does not hesitate,
He leaps across a five-bar gate.

"He's tumbled down! It's all my fault!"
Gasps Rupert. "He's too old to vault!"

Laughs Gaffer, "I'm not hurt one bit!
It's ages since I felt so fit."

"Thank'ee, it's been my lucky day!"
Then he goes prancing on his way.

In his excitement Gaffer Jarge makes larger hops across the field. "Tis magic, sure 'nough," he wheezes. "Forty year ago I used to think naught o' yon five-bar gate. Wonder if I could get over it now." He puts his hands on the top bar and next moment he is well across. "Oh, I say! I didn't mean you to do that!" cries Rupert anxiously as the old man tumbles over. "Are you hurt?" There is a pause and then to his great relief Gaffer, still lying on his back, gives him a slow smile. Hurrying over the gate to help the old man Rupert finds him looking very pleased with himself. "Shall I see you home?" Rupert asks. "Nay, haven't felt so spry this many a year," declares Gaffer Jarge. "Fancy me jumpin' gates! Glad you see'd me do it, young Rupert, else nobody would believe it. Now I'll jump towards home. Even if me old muscles let me down, tumblin' don't seem to hurt any more!" Rupert fetches the old man's stick and watches him as he goes hopping towards his cottage.

RUPERT SPRINGS EVEN HIGHER

Rupert is gaining weight again,
"I need more water, it is plain."

"There's someone moving, I feel sure!
I'll take a drink, then I'll explore."

"These rocks are nice! The top looks flat,
But could I jump as high as that?"

He swings his arms to launch himself,
And leaps on to the rocky shelf.

When his old friend seems safely on his way Rupert takes the jug back towards the little river. "That strange water has given Gaffer Jarge an unexpected treat, but we still don't know whether there really is magic in the spring," he murmurs. "Hello, I don't seem able to jump as high as I could. I'd better take a little more of that clear water." As he kneels by the spring he pauses and listens. "I could be sure I heard somebody moving near," he thinks. Rupert calls once or twice and moves around among the big reeds without finding anybody. "I'm sure I heard someone," he says. "Let me explore above the spring. My, what nice rocks these are. I believe there's a shelf up there. How I wish I could climb to it." Then he stops. "But I *can* get there," he mutters. "I could *jump* it!" He takes a little more of the sparkling water from the jug and, after one or two trial leaps, he launches himself upward with a terrific spring towards the shelf.

RUPERT ASTONISHES AN IMP

An Imp of Spring looks round in fright,
"How could a bear jump such a height?"

"Because of water that I drank,
Huge reeds are growing on the bank."

"The tiny river's just down there,
Its water made me light as air!"

"I must find out what's going on!"
The Imp exclaims, then he is gone.

Rupert's jumping power is now greater than he expects. He makes the shelf easily and lands on all fours. Almost at once he realises he is not alone. A small face is looking at him barely two feet away. "Oh dear, does this place belong to you?" says Rupert. "You're one of the Imps of Spring, aren't you? I wouldn't have jumped up here if I'd known you lived here." "Jumped? What do you mean?" demands the Imp. "No bear could jump so high." Rupert insists that he did jump up to the shelf. "There's a little tiny river down there," he says. "It's only a few yards long and there are huge reeds growing beside it. Bill Badger and I found the spring where it starts. The water tasted lovely and when we swallowed some of it we seemed to become as light as feathers. We could jump anywhere." The Imp of Spring listens and looks both astonished and worried at what he hears. Then without a word he leaps from the shelf and Rupert watches him going down . . . down.

RUPERT PROVES TO BE RIGHT

The Imp dips in a finger tip,
He stirs the pool, then takes a sip.

He springs back. "I must deal with this!
There's something very much amiss."

Says Rupert, "I forgot to tell,
Those reeds are very light as well."

"Light reeds!" The Imp darts through a crack,
"That clue has put me on the track!"

"That's the place," says Rupert, peering down from his perch. "That's the river. Now drink a little of it." The Imp of Spring stares at the running water, touches it and then takes a sip. Next minute he leaps from the rocks, soars high above the shelf and lands softly beside Rupert. "I wish you'd told us as soon as you first found you could jump like that, little bear," he says. "There's something very, very wrong with that water!" The anxious expression on the face of the Imp makes Rupert feel worried too. "I couldn't tell you sooner because I didn't know you were here," he says. "I told my parents and I gave some water to old Gaffer Jarge. He thought it was wonderful being able to jump again. And my Mummy thought those big reeds without weight were wonderful too." The Imp stares. "Light reeds, that's the clue!" he cries, and in a flash he has disappeared into a dark crack between two large boulders.

RUPERT ENTERS A WORK-ROOM

So Rupert follows, still in doubt,
But hoping he will soon find out.

"Hurry!" the Imp calls. "Come along!
Your clue has told me what is wrong."

"There's been a leak! Raise the alarm!
Then find it, ere it does more harm!"

In clouds of steam, and wearing masks,
More Imps are busy at their tasks.

"I wonder where that Imp has gone to and whether he wants me to follow," thinks Rupert. The adventure has become so interesting that he doesn't want it to stop without the mystery being explained. He squeezes through the crack in the rock. "My, nobody larger than I am could get through that crack," he murmurs. The Imp is waiting impatiently for him. "Come along! Hurry up!" he says, and leads the way up a rough stair-way winding first right and then left until he reaches a door. The Imp of Spring pushes the door and speaks urgently to somebody inside. "There's been a leak," he cries, "and unless we can find it there's going to be trouble." Following him through, Rupert sees other Imps in weird masks busily stirring bluish fluids in large cauldrons with pipes leading off in various directions. "Phew, this steam hurts my eyes and nose," Rupert splutters. "Whatever are they doing in all this awful steam? It's too much for me!"

RUPERT FORGETS HE IS LIGHT

" They've tried so hard for many days
To grow light wood with special sprays."

" Their newest mixtures, it would seem,
Have leaked into your little stream."

Still weightless, Rupert gives a jump,
He hits the roof with quite a bump.

The Imp says, " You're too light by far,
So sip this water! Here you are!"

"My, this steam is terrible!" says Rupert in a muffled voice. "I wonder you can stand it." "Oh, we get used to it," says the Imp. "These are some of our back-room boys and they are always experimenting in order to improve plants in spring. Just now they're trying to make mixtures to spray over them, so that some wood grows very hard and heavy and other wood grows soft and very light. Some of their newest mixtures must have leaked out and got into your tiny river!" When Rupert hears the Imp call him out of the steamy room he gladly hurries to obey, quite forgetting how light he still is, and he immediately bumps his head on the roof of the passage. "Ouch, I wish I really knew how all this will end!" he says. "I hardly dare take a step for fear of going too high." "I'll put you right," grins the Imp. "Pick yourself up and have a sip of this." He takes a beakerful of water from one of two basins and offers it to Rupert.

RUPERT CAN HARDLY FOLLOW

One sip, and Rupert feels a change,
"I'm getting heavier! How strange!"

Now he can hardly get ahead,
His feet feel just like lumps of lead!

"Here we treat plants with sprays and such,
We drench them well, but not too much."

"We can, by treating new young trees,
Grow soft or hard woods, as we please."

Rupert takes a sip from the beaker. "This has no more taste than the water in the little river," he declares. "Is it different? Stop a minute! It makes me feel different inside." "Yes, it will change you altogether," laughs the Imp. "No more bumping against the ceiling. Let's go now. You can help me discover the leak, if there is one." Rupert tries to start forward. "Hi, wait for me," he calls. "My feet feel as heavy as lead. I can hardly walk!" The Imp laughs again. "I told you that you couldn't jump to the ceiling after that other sip of water," he declares. "Perhaps it has slowed you down too much. Look, here's our testing room for hard and soft woods." Ahead of him Rupert sees different plants, some of them very like his own reeds, under some overhead sprinklers, while more of the Imp back-room boys, completely covered in waterproof clothes, are keeping watch and making sure the plants are well watered.

RUPERT BEGINS TO UNDERSTAND

Now Rupert is allowed to hold
Some treated plants. "That's hard," he's told.

"When fully grown, it will produce
Hard wood like this, for people's use."

More Imps are called, and form a group,
"Search for the leak!" Away they troop.

"That heavy water's made you slow,
Sip some light water, ere we go."

Rupert is so interested in the Imps' work that he is allowed to hold some of the treated plants, first a light branch and then a smaller one, much heavier, that he can hardly bend. "But what use are these?" he asks. "Not much until they become forest trees," says the Imp. "Then very soft wood and very hard wood are valuable. Come and look here." Round a corner is a pile of wood blocks. Rupert tries to lift a small one. "Whew, this is as heavy as a bar of iron!" he puffs. "I can scarcely hold it." Having satisfied Rupert's inquisitiveness the Imp gets on with his search. Calling a group of other Imps and back-room boys, he explains what he thinks must have happened and tells them to help in searching for the leak. "I'd like to help too," says Rupert, "but I should be terribly slow now that my feet are so hard to move." "H'm, you must have taken too much of that heavy water," says the Imp. "You need a sip of light water to put you right."

RUPERT KNEELS NEAR THE TAP

RUPERT KNEELS NEAR THE TAP

"The tap's in there, a beaker too,
It must be turned off after you!"

"That tap!" gasps Rupert, as he sips,
"It won't turn off! How fast it drips!"

He waves and calls, in eagerness,
"I think I've found the trouble, yes!"

"Water's been flowing, unawares,
Into a crevice!" he declares.

Looking for a sign marked "S" on the wall the Imp points into a cleft in the rock. "You'll find a tap with light water for making soft wood," he says. "Help yourself to a drop and be sure to turn the tap off firmly." Taking another beaker off the wall, Rupert quickly finds the place and has a taste of the light water. "Hello, the tap's dripping and the water's running down that crack," he says, trying to turn it off. However, he cannot turn it. "Oh my goodness! It's faulty! *It won't turn off!*" he exclaims. As soon as he finds that the water from the tap has made him light again Rupert skips out into the rocky passage in great excitement at his discovery. He bounces up and down, taking care not to hit the roof, and calls until some of the back-room boys and the other searchers hear him, and soon the Imp has come back to him. "What are you shouting about?" demands the Imp. "Just you look inside that cleft!" chuckles Rupert, "and see what I have found."

RUPERT SOLVES THE MYSTERY

*"You're right! It's trickling down that gap
Into your spring, straight from our tap!"*

*"Your tiny river has been filled
With secret mixture, as it spilled!"*

*"Such carelessness! You're all to blame!
How fortunate that Rupert came!"*

*The Imp leads Rupert from the cleft,
"They'll mend it! Now, it's time you left."*

Inside the cleft the Imp gazes at the dripping tap and at the water running away. "So that's the cause of all the trouble!" he gasps. "There's not a doubt of it. This is trickling into your spring and making your little river full of the wrong sort of water. Somebody's been very, very careless not to see it before. It must be turned off at the main and our mechanics shall mend it." Rupert smiles with relief as he follows the Imp out of the cleft. "I'm glad your worries are over," he says. Rupert watches while his little leader calls a group of the searchers together and lectures them. "You've all been most careless," he cries. "Not one of you has noticed the leak and our secrets might have been revealed to everybody. Rupert here has been jumping far too high. And he tells me an old man vaulted a five-bar gate after a sip of our light water! It must never happen again! Come on, Rupert." And away he goes along the passage.

RUPERT JUMPS OFF THE LEDGE

"You'll need some water of each kind,
To make your weight just right, you'll find."

"Sip some light water first of all,
Then jump, and you will float, not fall."

Rupert obeys, then springs, and soon
Drifts down as light as a balloon.

The Imp, a beaker in each hand,
Takes off, and gently comes to land.

The Imp of Spring is now very cheerful. "It's a good thing you let us know about the change in that little river, Rupert," he says. "It might have caused all sorts of trouble if our secrets had flowed down there much longer. Now you'd better get along home. I've brought a little of both kinds of water, to make sure you're just an ordinary little bear when I send you away." Soon they are through the crack and out on the shelf. "Take another sip of the light water before you jump," says the Imp. Rupert makes one or two slight jumps to make sure he is practically no weight at all. Then he launches himself from the ledge and floats down to the rocks and the tall reeds. "Wait for me," the Imp calls. "I can't allow you to go home like that." Next minute the little creature is dropping gently down after him, holding a beaker carefully in each hand. He lands as lightly as a feather, without spilling a drop of water.

RUPERT TRIES EACH BEAKER

" *You're light as air, and no mistake!*
Heavy water's the thing to take! "

" *Too heavy now? Don't be perplexed!* "
The Imp laughs, " *Try light water next!* "

Rupert tries some of each, once more,
At length, he feels just as before.

" *Long reeds are all that I can get,*
I've found no pussy-willow yet. "

The Imp bounces several times before he finally comes to rest beside Rupert. "Now then, we must make you just as your Mummy knows you," he says. "You're as light as a balloon. Have a drop of this heavy water." Rupert takes a little and looks thoughtful. "There's magic in this," he murmurs. "My feet feel like lead now, just as they did up in that long corridor." "Then have a drop from the other one," says the Imp. "You see, I *must* make you exactly the proper weight!" At length Rupert declares that he feels just as he was before he first found the little river. "Right," says the Imp. "And, now that we've stopped that leak, there's only ordinary water in this spring, so you'd better run off home." Rupert gathers two of the long reeds. "My Mummy really wanted pussy-willow, but I found these instead and she liked them, so I'll give her two more. Good-bye." Hardly has he set off on the way home when he hears his name called.

RUPERT SPREADS THE NEWS

"*You've helped us, so we'll plant, at dawn,*
Some pussy-willow by your lawn."

Then Rupert, making for the green,
Meets Bill, returning to the scene.

"*There's just plain water in that spring,*
Some day I'll tell you everything!"

Now Gaffer stands and waves his stick,
"*Hey, young Rupert! Do'ee come quick!*"

Returning uphill Rupert finds the Imp holding the little jug. "Oh, I forgot that," he says. "I meant to take some magic water to Mummy." "You say she wants some pussy-willow," says the Imp. "Well, I'd like to do you a good turn, so by tomorrow I'll see that a plant of it is growing in your Mummy's garden." Thanking him, Rupert starts happily homeward. He meets Bill Badger who is on his way up and who just misses seeing the Imp leaping back on to the shelf. "Hello, are you going home?" asks Bill. "Why are you carrying an empty jug?" "I wanted to take some of that magic water back to Mummy," says Rupert, "but there's none in the spring now and there never will be any more. If you want some of these light reeds you'd better take them while there are any left. I'll tell you all the story one day. Good-bye." As he runs down the hill he sees Gaffer Jarge, and the old man waves, clearly wanting him to stop and have a talk with him.

RUPERT AMUSES THE OLD MAN

"Yon magic water eased my legs,
Gimme another drop!" he begs.

"The magic's gone, and can't return,
As you and Simon there shall learn."

"I knew it was too good to last!"
Calls Gaffer, not a bit downcast.

"Tomorrow, from your sitting-room,
You'll see some pussy-willow bloom!"

"Hey, young Rupert," chuckles Gaffer Jarge as they meet. "Do 'ee gimme another drop of that magic spring water. Never felt so spry for years I haven't, but the effect's wearing off now." "Oh, I'm very sorry!" says Rupert. "The magic was leaking out of the Imps' workshop. Now it's shut off and there'll never be any more." "Can't understand a word of it," croaks Gaffer Jarge. "Never mind, it was too good to last. Now gimme your shoulder and help me home." Just then Simple

Simon joins them. Rupert tells his story and soon Simon knows about the light reeds that he had found. "Well, well, you and your pals are always playin' tricks on me, young Rupert," wheezes Gaffer Jarge, "but I must say I enjoyed this one! Now you run on your way. Simon here will let me lean on him and help me home. And no more jumpin' over gates, more's the pity!" So Rupert scampers off with his light reeds and his empty jug, and tells his story all over again to Mrs. Bear.

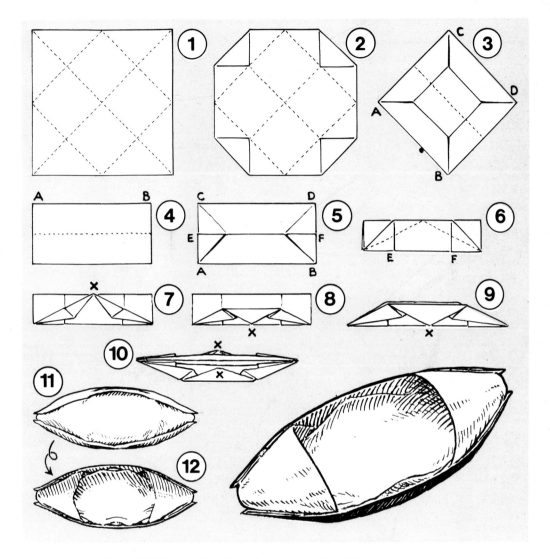

RUPERT'S CHINESE BOAT

When you read the next story you will find that one of Rupert's friends is a little Chinese girl. Here is a model of a boat called a Sampan in which she enjoys sailing when she is in China.

You will need a square of paper. Fold opposite corners together both ways to find the middle point, then fold all corners to the centre so that when opened the creases look like Fig. 1. Now fold all corners neatly to the last creases you have made (Fig. 2) and fold them over again to make Fig. 3. Take the side AB across to CD, press firmly (Fig. 4) and bring AB down to the bottom line as in Fig. 5. Fold CD down at the back and bring down the points E and F as in Fig. 6. Then bring the new, shallow top corners forward using the sloping dotted lines. The folds are now getting rather thick so keep your finger firmly on E and F to prevent them from slipping down (Fig. 7). Carefully bring the new corner X down to the bottom line (Fig. 8) and repeat Figs. 6, 7 and 8 behind to make Fig. 9.

Turn the model the other way up (Fig. 10), hold the points X and the nearest thickness of paper between the finger and thumb of each hand and pull them apart, slowly and steadily turning the whole thing inside out (Fig. 11). Turn it over and there is your boat (Fig. 12). To complete the Sampan pull up the flaps at each end to look like awnings or "cabins".

RUPERT and the

RUPERT JOINS THREE FRIENDS

As Christmas-time draws near again,
Rupert is deep in thought, it's plain.

"Hi, Algy, Podgy! You look glad!
But why is Gregory so sad?"

CHRISTMAS is quite near and, although the excitement of preparing has begun, Rupert is walking quietly through the village, lost in thought and paying no attention to the brightly decorated shops filled with gifts. Just round a corner he finds his pals Algy Pug, Podgy Pig and Gregory Guineapig gazing at a shop window. Two of them seem very cheerful. "Hi, Rupert! I've just made up my mind what I want for Christmas,"

says Podgy. "I've decided to ask Santa Claus for a trumpet." "And I'm going to write to him for some roller skates," Algy smiles. "At first I wanted ice skates, but I could only use them when there's thick ice on the pond. Roller skates are grand fun at any time of year." But to Rupert's surprise little Gregory doesn't say a word. Almost at once the little guineapig, still silent, heaves a long sigh, then turns and moves away from the group.

THINKING CAP

It is a magic cap belonging to Tigerlily's Daddy, the Chinese Conjurer. Rupert hopes it will be a way of finding out what one of his chums wants for Christmas. The result puzzles the little bear, so he has a chat with the very wise old Gipsy Granny.

RUPERT ASKS ABOUT GREGORY

*"He just can't think of anything
That he'd like Santa Claus to bring."*

*"H'm, I've got lots of things in mind,
My problem's which to choose, I find!"*

Rupert gazes after the little guineapig, who is walking away slowly and sadly. "We can't cheer him up at all," says Podgy. "He hasn't smiled once since we've been with him." "Why is he so quiet?" asks Rupert. "It's not like Gregory to be unhappy. Usually he won't stop chattering and it's hard to get a word in. Isn't he feeling well?" "It isn't that!" laughs Podgy. "The poor fellow's worried because, try as he will, he can't think of anything

he really wants from Santa Claus. And there isn't much time left for him to make up his mind. If he doesn't look sharp Christmas will be over and then it will be too late." And still chuckling, he and Algy move off, leaving Rupert more thoughtful than ever. "H'm, yes, and I'm nearly in the same fix as little Gregory," he mutters. "There are lots of things I would like, but I can't decide what I want most of all for Christmas."

RUPERT DISCOVERS THE REASON

"I'd like to help, I've heard what's wrong!"
Calls Rupert, hurrying along.

"I think and think—I do indeed!—
To find a Christmas gift I need."

Calls Tigerlily from the slope,
"You both not feeling sad, I hope."

She listens with a gentle smile,
"New problem! Let me t'ink awhile!"

Rupert hurries after his gloomy pal. "I say, Podgy has told me your trouble," he calls. "The time is getting short for writing to Santa Claus. Perhaps we can help each other." "It's no good," moans Gregory. "I think and I think and I still have no notion of what I want for Christmas." "But surely, after all that thinking there must be some idea in your head!" says Rupert. "I doubt it," says Gregory. "Anyway, it won't come out!" Rupert is just going to tell Gregory that he too has difficulty about what to ask from Santa Claus when there is a cheery call, and their friend Tigerlily hurries up the slope. "Allo, 'allo," cries the little Chinese girl. "Why you both not look happy on so fine, sunny morning? What matter now?" Rupert quickly tells her why Gregory looks so miserable and Tigerlily smiles. "So little guinea-pig no can t'ink," she says. "That velly interesting, velly new problem. Now you wait while me t'ink. P'raps me can help!"

RUPERT CALLS ON THE CONJURER

Says Tigerlily, with a frown,
"P'raps him t'ink best upside down!"

"Can't stand on head? Then me suggest
We ask my Daddy. Him know best."

Past trees that still bear fruit they roam,
And enter her strange Chinese home.

The Conjurer, a clever man,
Agrees to help them, if he can.

Rupert watches the little Chinese girl as she stands and looks at Gregory. Then she speaks. "Guineapig no can t'ink when standing up," she murmurs. "P'raps if he stands on his head he t'ink better, yes?" "But I can't stand on my head!" cries Gregory. "My arms are too short. I always topple over!" "H'm, then we must find out why guineapig no can t'ink," says Tigerlily. "That too difficult for me. Come, we go ask my Daddy. He velly clever." And she leads them away towards the Conjurer's house. Soon the little party is moving through Tigerlily's strange garden, where leaves and fruit appear on the trees although it is winter time. Rupert and Gregory want to stop and look, but the little girl hurries them indoors to a room where the Chinese Conjurer is at work. "Oh honourable Daddy," she says, bowing politely, "me bring you problem. Gregory Guineapig no can t'ink. You please tell him why, yes?" The Conjurer gazes in surprise. Then he rises from his chair.

RUPERT'S CHUM NEEDS A TEST

"Guineapig noddle fit and well!
Why no can t'ink, me cannot tell."

"Try Chinese t'inking cap on him,
It full of magic to the brim."

"'Put on your thinking cap,' they say,
But I've not seen one, till today!"

"Use t'inking cap to choose your gift,
The magic in it velly swift!"

Turning Gregory round the Conjurer passes his hands over his head and while he mutters strange Chinese spells small sparks begin to flash. "H'm, no can understand," he whispers. "Nothing wrong with Guineapig noddle. Why can he no t'ink?" "Oh, I'm not that bad!" says Gregory. "I can think about most things, but when I try to think what Christmas presents to ask Santa Claus for, nothing happens!" The Conjurer unlocks a cupboard, picks up something, and returns with a cloth object in his hand. Rupert takes the object and peers at it. "Why, it's a sort of cap, isn't it?" he murmurs. "Yes, that Chinese t'inking cap!" says the Conjurer. "Him full of Chinese magic." "A thinking cap!" cries Rupert. "My Daddy has often told me to put on my thinking cap, but I never knew there really was such a thing! May I see if it fits me?" "No," replies the Conjurer. "Let Guineapig put on cap and t'ink hard about presents and Santa Claus and soon he get plenty ideas."

RUPERT WAITS FOR THE RESULT

"It gives my head a tickly thrill!"
But Gregory is told, "Stand still!"

"Good," says the man, "now thoughts escape!"
He peers into each misty shape.

"Empty, all empty, I'm afraid!"
He whispers, as the thought clouds fade.

"Nothing in noddle! Velly strange!
Me solly, magic no can change."

Rupert obediently gives the Thinking Cap to his pal, though Gregory looks nervous. "Oh dear, it makes my head tickle," he quavers. "Never mind," says the Conjurer. "Do not talk. Only stand still and t'ink hard about Santa Claus." In the silence that follows he waves his wand, and gradually misty shapes appear over Gregory's head. "Good, good," says the man. "Now he t'ink. Now we *see* what he t'ink." "Oh my!" gasps Rupert. "Are those clouds really his thoughts?" The Conjurer gazes fixedly at the misty shapes and Gregory, catching sight of them, looks up startled, so that the Thinking Cap falls off. One after another the mists fade and vanish. Then the man silently lifts him on to the table. "It true!" he whispers. "Me never before meet guineapig with *nothing* in noddle! I can do no more for him." "Oh dear," says Rupert. "Does that mean that he still has no ideas for Christmas?" "Yes, yes. It great pity," says the Conjurer. "Goodbye. Me velly solly."

RUPERT HAS A NEW FOOTBALL

"Cheer up! Let Santa make the choice!"
Says Rupert, in a hopeful voice.

"As neither of us wrote for things,
Let's wait and see what Santa brings."

"That parcel's round, just like a ball!
I'll open that one first of all."

"I didn't write for one, myself,
I've got one, somewhere on a shelf."

Tigerlily sees the two pals part of the way home and Gregory is gloomier than ever after the Conjurer's failure to help him think. "Don't be too sad," says Rupert as they part. "I haven't written to Santa Claus either. But my trouble is that I want so many things and I can't think which present to write for. I tell you what, let's just wait and see what Santa brings us. He may know what we want, better than we do ourselves. And I'll come over on Christmas morning to see what

you've got." And so they part. On Christmas morning Rupert wakes and sits up. Before he can look at his full stocking he spies a large round parcel at the foot of the bed. It is tied with lots of string and inside is a lovely ball. Hurriedly he dresses and, running from the room, finds Mrs. Bear is already up. "I say, Mummy, look at this grand ball!" he cries. "I wonder why Santa Claus chose it for me. I already have a football about this size, though I haven't used it this season."

RUPERT SEARCHES THE ATTIC

Still puzzling, Rupert goes in search,
He lifts the old ball from its perch.

" It's burst!" he gasps, in great surprise,
" So Santa knew—he's very wise."

" Dear Santa knew just what to send,"
He smiles, then runs to tell his friend.

" Here's Gregory himself! Oh, good!"
And Rupert meets him by the wood.

Rupert is puzzling over the arrival of the ball. "I know what I'll do," he thinks. "I'll get my football and compare it with the new one and see which is the better." He searches until he finds, in the lumber room, the older ball. "Why, it's burst!" he gasps. "And the cover's all cracked. It's no use any more. I see what's happened. Santa Claus did know what I wanted better than I knew myself! This is marvellous! I must go and tell Mummy at once." Mrs. Bear is delighted that Rupert, after all, has got the present that he wanted. "It just shows," he says, "that sometimes you need not write to Santa Claus before Christmas. He must be a very wise old gentleman." Rupert quickly puts on his scarf. "Gregory Guineapig didn't write either," he says. "He promised to show me his present, but I can't wait to see if he has been as lucky as I have. May I go and meet him?" He scampers off and presently, as he crosses the Common, he sees his pal coming towards him.

RUPERT UNWRAPS THE BOX

"Is that your present? Show me it!
The box looks fine, I must admit."

"It's very light," He lifts the lid,
"It's empty! Well I never did!"

"He's feeling worse, and with good cause!
His problem's baffled Santa Claus!"

"Hello," calls Algy, "what's amiss?
We've never seen him quite like this."

Rupert greets his pal eagerly. "I say, isn't it wonderful!" he cries. "I've had just the present I wanted. Santa Claus knew what to bring although we didn't write. What did he bring you? Is that your present?" To his surprise the little guineapig looks gloomier than ever. "Yes, I promised to show it to you. Here it is," says Gregory. Then he bursts into tears. In some bewilderment Rupert removes the paper. "The box is very light," he murmurs. Then he lifts off the lid. "Why it's *empty*!" he

exclaims. For some minutes the two friends stare at each other in silence. Then the little guineapig wanders away and sits down. "This is just terrible," thinks Rupert. "The problem must be pretty bad if even Santa Claus doesn't know what he wants!" At that moment he is hailed by cheery voices as Algy and Podgy come to greet him. "Hi, what's going on?" demands Algy. "Why is Gregory looking so grumpy? Don't tell us that he is still miserable." "Yes, worse than ever," says Rupert.

RUPERT DOES HIS VERY BEST

"An empty box! Is that what came?"
Cries Podgy. "What a dreadful shame!"

"Let's try to help him!" Down they sink,
Then solemnly they think and think.

"I cannot think for other folk,
Just thinking for myself's no joke!"

Says Rupert, when their pals have gone,
"It's time to take you home. Come on!"

Algy and Podgy are astonished that even Christmas has not made Gregory cheer up, so Rupert fetches the empty box and tells them all about it. "But this is extraordinary!" says Podgy. "I've never heard of anybody getting a Christmas present of nothing! He must want something. Everybody wants *something*!" "Well, he doesn't know what he wants," says Rupert. "Let's try to help him think." So they all sit on the boulder and begin to think and think. At length Algy and Podgy get up. "It's no use," says Podgy. "I'm no use at thinking for other people. It's as much as I can do to think for myself!" "And I'm sure I'm no better," says Algy. "We'd better go on our way." "Oh dear," sighs Rupert. "It does seem a shame that Gregory should be the only one of us not to have a present. He can share mine if he likes but that's not quite the same thing. Anyway, I'll see him home now." He takes the little guineapig's hand while Algy and Podgy go the other way.

RUPERT GOES BACK TO TIGERLILY

"*Eh, where?*" *asks Gregory, and stops,*
"*I can't see over those bush tops.*"

"*Oh dear, I wish I weren't so short!*"
He mutters, with a grumpy snort.

Says Rupert, "*I've a new idea,*
Hi, Tigerlily! Come down here!"

"*Guineapig no could t'ink, and so*
He not get any plesent, no?"

On their way to the little guineapig's house Rupert comes to a halt and looks over the top of a bush. "I say, that's the Conjurer's house!" he exclaims. "That's given me an idea. Let's go and . . ." "Eh, what? Where's the house?" Gregory interrupts grumpily. "Oh, I do wish I wasn't so small and I could see over the top of things as you do! I'm the smallest of all of us." "Never mind," says Rupert, interrupting in his turn. "Come round the bush. We'll leave your box here on this side and look for Tigerlily." Gregory does not understand what Rupert's new idea is, but he allows himself to be led into the grounds of the Conjurer's house. "Ah, there is Tigerlily herself, on the terrace," says Rupert. "She must have seen us and has come to meet us." When the little Chinese girl has joined them Rupert tells her of Gregory's disappointment. "Ah, guineapig get no plesent," says Tigerlily. "Yes, yes. That what me expect. But, please, why you fetch him back here?"

38

RUPERT HOPES THE PLAN WORKS

"Please try the Thinking Cap on me,
And let me think for Gregory!"

"Hush, Daddy busy, not make sound!
Me see if cap can still be found."

The girl runs softly as a mouse,
And brings the cap back from the house.

"Keep trying, Rupert! Don't lose heart!"
Then Tigerlily gives a start.

Rupert quickly tells Tigerlily of his new idea. "Poor Gregory couldn't think of anything he wanted, even when he wore your Daddy's wonderful cap," he says. "Today Algy and Podgy and I have been trying to help him, but we've had no luck. Now do you suppose that if I wore the Thinking Cap and tried very hard I could think for him?" The little girl pauses. "My honourable Daddy velly busy," she murmurs, "but it good idea. Maybe me can find cap. You and guineapig stay here and keep velly, velly quiet." In a few minutes the little Chinese girl trots back holding out the Thinking Cap. Rupert puts it on while Gregory looks on expectantly. "Now t'ink hard. T'ink about guineapig," murmurs Tigerlily, and she begins to wave her wand over and around the cap. "Ow, it does feel funny," Rupert mutters. "The more I try to think the more it tickles." "That's just what it did to me," says Gregory. "Please keep on trying."

RUPERT WON'T GIVE UP YET

"Now we see cloud with something in!
It look like two sticks, faint and thin."

"All vanish!" Tigerlily cries,
"Me not see what you t'ink," she sighs.

"You all had gifts, mine hasn't come,"
And Gregory looks very glum.

"He's right! We all got splendid toys,"
Then Rupert hears a rustling noise.

Just as Rupert is getting up Gregory gives a gasp. "There it is," he cries. "You're thinking of something!" And, sure enough, a thin cloud appears over Rupert's head. "Yes, and there's something in it," says Tigerlily. "It looks like two sticks, very faint and . . . oh dear, now it all vanish. Nothing left. No good, me cannot tell what you t'ink." "Phew, thinking is awfully hard work," sighs Rupert. "I really can't do any more." After thanking Tigerlily the two friends make their way from the Conjurer's house and towards Nutwood. Both are silent and not very happy. At length Gregory stops. "I can find my way alone from here," he says moodily. "You've been a good pal to try to help me, but I won't bother you any more. Christmas has gone and I just shan't get a present." And off he wanders. However, Rupert doesn't like to give up the problem. "There must be *somebody* with some ideas somewhere," he thinks. All at once some sound catches his ear and he turns and listens.

RUPERT GATHERS SOME TWIGS

"Hi, Rollo! It was you I heard!"
He tells the boy what has occurred.

"You thought too hard! That's a mistake,
Do something else, you need a break."

"If you keep busy, and forget,
You'll think of something, even yet."

Towards the gipsy camp they trot,
"What splendid bundles we have got!"

The noise that Rupert heard is repeated and, moving towards it, he spies Rollo the gipsy boy collecting dead wood in a thicket. "Hello, little bear," he calls cheerily. "You're looking very solemn. What's the matter? Did you have too much plum pudding at Christmas?" "Don't be silly," says Rupert. "It's something much more puzzling." And he tells the strange story of Gregory and Santa Claus and the Thinking Cap. "Well, that certainly is odd," says Rollo. "I've never heard of that problem before." After a few moments Rollo's face brightens. "While you were trying so hard to think what Gregory would like for Christmas you couldn't get any ideas," he says. "Now suppose you make yourself busy. Then an idea may come when you're not trying at all." "Well, that's a new notion," says Rupert. "I'll help you with your job." And he runs about collecting twigs, until they both have good bundles, and then set off to the gipsy camp.

RUPERT'S STORY IS HEARD

"Please stay," the gipsy boy implores,
"My Granny likes odd tales like yours."

"Well, tell me what it's all about,"
Says Granny. "Mind, leave nothing out."

"Gregory wished he weren't so small?
He made no other wish at all?"

She moves away across the grass,
How silently the moments pass!

As they approach Rollo's caravan Rupert sighs. "Well, I've finished that job," he says, "and still no idea has come for helping Gregory. I'd better go home." "No, wait a minute," says Rollo. "Now that you're here you'd better stay and see my Granny. She knows lots and lots of things and she likes odd stories like that one of yours." At the sound of their voices the old lady comes forward. "Well, little bear, so you've a problem, eh?" she smiles. "Well, tell Granny all about it and mind you leave nothing out." As Rollo has expected, the Gipsy Granny is very interested in Rupert's tale. "Tell me, little bear," she says, "have you never heard your friend, the guineapig, wish for *anything*?" "Well," laughs Rupert, "today he said he wished he were not so small, when I looked over a bush and he couldn't. But that's got nothing to do with Santa Claus and Christmas presents, has it?" To his surprise the old lady makes no reply and moves thoughtfully away from them.

RUPERT LISTENS TO GRANNY

"Two sticks were seen, but nothing more,
Above the Thinking Cap you wore?"

"She's thought of something, I suspect!
Wait, you'll soon see if I'm correct."

"The Thinking Cap has told us right,"
Says Gipsy Granny, in delight.

"Send Gregory to see her now!
She'll help him, though I can't think how."

After a short silence the Gipsy Granny turns back. "Tell me again what Tigerlily saw in the little cloud when you had that Thinking Cap on," she demands. "Well, she thought she saw two lines that might have been sticks," says Rupert. "But they were very faint and soon vanished and she could make nothing of them." Again the old lady moves away in silence. "You'd better wait a bit," says Rollo. "She always behaves like this when she has an idea. I think you're in luck." Granny soon stops and faces Rupert with a slow smile. "Yes, I know what to do now," she says softly. "You are a clever little bear. When you were wearing your friend's Thinking Cap you solved your friend's problem, though you didn't know it at the time. Tell that little guineapig to come and see me at once." And without explaining any more she walks away. "I told you that my Granny would get an idea." Rollo laughs at Rupert's puzzled face. "You send Gregory straight here."

43

RUPERT PUZZLES THE GUINEAPIG

"Hi!" Rupert, running very fast,
Catches his gloomy pal at last.

"Quick, Rollo's Granny's sent for you!
She knows just what you want! It's true!"

"You'd better go without delay!"
Warns Rupert, then he trots away.

"Cloth cap? Small clouds with thoughts inside?"
Now Mummy listens, open-eyed.

Rupert cheers up at the thought that Gregory may be helped after all, and, although he cannot imagine how it will be done, he hurries away. The little guineapig has sauntered so slowly and moodily that Rupert soon catches him before he reaches home. "I've told that Gipsy Granny about you," he pants breathlessly. "And you're to go and see her at once. She says she knows what it was that you couldn't think of before Christmas." "But how can she?" Gregory gasps in surprise. "She doesn't even know me!" Gregory still gazes doubtfully at his pal. "Surely nobody can help me to think after all we've tried." "Old gipsies are terribly clever," says Rupert, "so don't forget to go as I told you." And he trots away to share the mystery with his Mummy. "The Gipsy Granny declares she knows what Gregory wants because of what I thought when I wore the Thinking Cap," he says. "But how can she? Neither Tiger-lily nor I could make head or tail of it!"

RUPERT BREAKS OFF HIS GAME

"New Year already," Rupert says,
"I've not seen Gregory for days."

"Gregory never joins our games,
He keeps his distance!" Bill exclaims.

Now Rupert stares, alert and tense,
"There's someone moving by that fence!"

"Hi, Gregory! Why keep away?
Did Gipsy Granny help, that day?"

When the excitements of Christmas are over time passes quickly. New Year comes and Rupert begins to tear the days off the new calendar on the wall. "I wonder why Gregory doesn't come and tell me if he visited the gipsies," he thinks. Taking the ball that Santa Claus has sent him he joins his pals. "I say, you chaps," he says. "Have any of you seen Gregory since Christmas?" "Why, yes," says Bill. "He goes into the wood sometimes, but for some reason he goes the other way when he sees us!" The pals are all puzzled at the way Gregory has kept himself aloof from them. However, they soon forget him in the fun of the game of football. All at once Rupert catches sight of a small figure near a hedge and, breaking from the game, he runs to the slope. "Hi, Gregory," he calls. "Where have you been? Why do you keep away from us? Have you seen the Gipsy Granny?" To his surprise the little guineapig only looks at him with a smile, says nothing and goes on walking.

RUPERT PAUSES ON THE WAY

Gregory turns his back awhile,
"Perhaps," he answers, with a smile.

"He's smiling! Something's happened, yes!
But what it is, I cannot guess."

Days fly, until their schooltime comes,
Then Rupert sets out with his chums.

"You chaps go on," he says, "I'll wait
For Gregory, I shan't be late."

Rupert is now thoroughly inquisitive as he trots beside the little guineapig. "Well, did you go to see the gipsies?" he repeats. "I may have done," murmurs Gregory, still with that smile, and not another word will he say. At length Rupert runs back to the others. "This is weird!" he explains. "I don't know what's come over him! Anyway, he's not as gloomy as he was. He's actually smiling." "Maybe he has at last thought of what he would have liked for Christmas," suggests Algy.

"But, if so, why not tell us?" Soon the holidays are finished. On the first day of school Bill and Podgy call for Rupert. "I still haven't seen any more of Gregory," says the little bear. "We're bound to see him today. Perhaps he will tell us what he's been doing." On the way they fall in with Freddy Fox and Algy, and then Rupert pauses. "This is where I often wait for Gregory," he says. "He's sometimes rather slow. You chaps go on and when he comes I'll hurry him up."

RUPERT STARES IN AMAZEMENT

As he stands waiting, all on edge,
"Cooee!" a voice calls from the hedge.

"Gregory!" gasps the little bear,
"How ever did you get up there?"

"Look, Rollo made these stilts of mine!
His Granny thought of them! They're fine."

"Although I've tumbled once or twice,
I think stilt-walking's jolly nice!"

When the others have gone Rupert waits quietly, looking across the country towards Gregory's cottage. "There isn't a sign of him," he mutters. "I wonder if he can have gone ahead of us?" At that moment a "Cooee!" sounds quite near, and, turning slowly, Rupert sees Gregory's face smiling above a bush. "My, how you made me jump!" he gasps. "What are you doing? How have you got up there? Are you standing on somebody's shoulders?" Hurrying round the bushes Rupert

stops in astonishment. "Well, how do you like my stilts?" cries the little guineapig. "They're just what I wanted for Christmas, although I didn't know it at the time. The Gipsy Granny thought of them for me and Rollo made them. Aren't gipsies clever! Now I can see over big bushes, and I shan't be the smallest person in Nutwood any more!" In his excitement he topples off them and laughs, but Rupert picks up a stilt. He looks at it thoughtfully, as an idea dawns on him.

RUPERT HURRIES ON AHEAD

*"Those two sticks seen in my thought cloud
Meant stilts!" And Rupert feels quite proud.*

*"Granny was sharp enough to know,"
He tells his chum. "Come on, let's go."*

*Into the school-house Rupert flies,
"Gregory's coming, sir!" he cries.*

*"Can that be him?" The chums stare hard,
"He must have grown at least a yard!"*

Rupert is sure his idea is right. "Don't you remember?" he says. "When I wore the Thinking Cap Tigerlily saw what looked like two sticks in the cloud. Only the Gipsy Granny was clever enough to know that they meant stilts!" "Well, anyway, they're jolly good!" cries Gregory. "I've been keeping quiet about them until Rollo taught me how to use them. You're the first of my pals to see them. Now come on." Scrambling on to a tree stump he mounts the stilts and is off towards school. In spite of his pride in his stilts Gregory is still rather slow, so Rupert leaves him. "I'd better run ahead and tell Dr. Chimp that you're coming," he says. The school is assembling when he arrives. "Please, sir," he calls breathlessly, "Gregory won't be long. He was just behind me and . . . why, look, there he is!" And, sure enough, the head of the little guineapig appears, bobbing through the window. "B-but is *that* Gregory?" the master gasps. "How has he grown so tall?"

RUPERT SENDS HIS THANKS

"Stilts!" gasps the master, in relief,
"I thought you'd grown beyond belief!"

In schooltime little work is done,
Then everyone joins in the fun.

"Oh, Rollo! You're a clever boy!
The gift you've made has brought such joy!"

"Now Gregory's our tallest chap,
Thanks to the Chinese Thinking Cap!"

Little work is done in school this morning. When Gregory comes noisily in on his stilts there is great excitement and everybody, even the master, wants to hear the story of his much-delayed Christmas present. Afterwards he good-naturedly lets all his pals try the stilts. One by one they come a cropper and meanwhile he talks to Tigerlily. "The two sticks that appeared when Rupert wore the Thinking Cap must have been stilts," he says. "Do tell your Daddy that its magic worked right for me." Outside the school Rollo is waiting to walk home with the pals. "I say, you're jolly clever to have made those things for Gregory!" Rupert exclaims. "But fancy your keeping quiet about them for so long! And your Granny is wonderful to have thought of them!" "Well, little bear, you gave her the two clues that put her on the right track," laughs the boy. Then they say goodbye and go their different ways, leaving Rupert to explain to his Mummy the strange sight of a guineapig on stilts!

Rupert visits Pussyville to buy a plate like the one Mummy has dropped. That same day there is another mishap and it seems Rupert has spent his savings in vain. Then a stranger arrives and reveals a secret which brings much joy to the little bear.

RUPERT WONDERS WHAT IS WRONG

"What's that?" breathes Rupert. "Something fell, In Mummy's kitchen, I can tell."

There Mummy sits, quite dazed and weak, She holds her head and does not speak.

IT is a quiet day in the Bear household. Although the weather is windy and unsettled, Mr. Bear is pottering in the garden, but Rupert chooses to stay indoors and play with his bricks. He is wondering if there is anything else he ought to be doing when all at once he hears the sound of something breaking. "Mummy's in the kitchen," he thinks. "I'd better go and see what she has dropped." Hurrying through the passage he enters the kitchen and finds Mrs. Bear sitting in a chair and looking very dazed. "What's the matter, Mummy?" asks Rupert anxiously. "Aren't you feeling well?" He gazes at the floor and sees the broken remains of a plate. "Oh, what a pity!" he cries. "That's one of your favourites. Shall I get the pan and brush and sweep up those pieces?" He waits for a reply, but Mrs. Bear is holding her head and doesn't answer.

the
PLATE

RUPERT HURRIES OUT TO MR. BEAR

"Quick, Daddy!" Rupert gives a call,
"It's Mummy! She's not well at all!"

"Oh dear, the room just seemed to spin,"
Sighs Mummy, as they hurry in.

Again Rupert speaks to his Mummy, but she remains so curiously silent that he becomes anxious and runs into the garden to call Mr. Bear. "Can you come, Daddy?" he says. "Mummy doesn't look very well. She's in the kitchen, but she won't say a word to me. She broke one of her favourite plates and perhaps it has upset her badly." Mr. Bear does not delay and, hastily putting aside his gardening tools, he follows Rupert into the house. Mrs. Bear turns her head as they enter the kitchen. "Oh dear, I don't know what happened," she says rather shakily. "Quite suddenly I felt giddy and I think I dropped a plate." "Well, don't worry about it," says Mr. Bear in a soothing voice. "I expect you're feeling tired. You mustn't do any more work today. Rupert, will you get Mummy's hot-water bottle and we'll make her as comfy as we can. I'm sure she will feel better after a rest."

RUPERT LEAVES A MESSAGE

Says Daddy, "*You must stay in bed,*
We two will run the house instead."

"*Fetch Dr. Lion. Take along*
A note from me, to say what's wrong."

"*The Doctor's on his rounds! I'll try*
And catch him as he passes by."

"*Oh dear,*" *puffs Rupert.* "*This is grim,*
I hope she gets my note to him."

Mrs. Bear is made as comfortable as possible and then Rupert and his Daddy bring a cup of tea to her. "You must stay here for the present," says Mr. Bear. "Rupert and I can manage things quite well for a while." However, when they have left her he looks uneasy. "She ought to have a long rest," he murmurs, "but I know she won't stay in bed just because I tell her to. You'd better fetch Dr. Lion." And, getting some paper, he writes a note for Rupert to take to the doctor.

Rupert sets off without delay. "It would be awful if Mummy were to be really ill," he thinks. "I don't know what we should do." But though he races to Dr. Lion's house, the doctor has already started on his rounds, so Rupert hands the note to the little maid and tells her just how urgent it is. She says that the doctor may be passing the house again in a few minutes and promises to try to stop him. "I wonder what I'd better do next," thinks Rupert as he runs home.

RUPERT LIKES BILL'S IDEA

"Rupert! What's up?" his pals exclaim.
"Your Mummy's ill? Oh, what a shame!"

"A gift," says Bill, "would bring delight,
And help to put your Mummy right."

Thinks Rupert, "That seems good advice!
I must buy Mummy something nice."

The Doctor is already there,
He says, "She needs a change of air."

As Rupert hurries past the shops he hears his name being called and turns to see his pals Bill Badger and Algy Pug, who are wanting him to play with them. Crossing the road he quickly explains why he cannot join them for a game. "Oo, I'm sorry your Mummy is not well," says Bill. "Why don't you buy her a present to make her happy? My Daddy says that people get better faster if they are happy." "Jolly good idea!" Rupert cries. "I wish I knew just what she would like." Leaving his pals Rupert makes his way homeward deep in thought. "I wonder what I could get for Mummy," he muses. "She doesn't need sweets if she is not well and she doesn't play with toys and she looks too tired to want to read books. Perhaps Daddy can suggest something." When his own cottage comes in sight he sees that a car is outside so he scampers forward, but at the gate he pauses, for Mr. Bear and Dr. Lion are standing in the garden and are talking together very seriously.

RUPERT SWEEPS UP THE PIECES

"Now Mrs. Bear must have some rest,
A warmer place would suit her best."

Thinks Rupert, "I must do my part,
I'll clear these bits up, for a start."

"That was a nice old plate we had,
One like it would make Mummy glad!"

He gives his money-box a shake,
"Daddy will know how much to take."

At length Dr. Lion prepares to leave. "Mrs. Bear has been working too hard," he says. "She must have a proper rest. She'd get better much more quickly if you sent her away to the South in the warmer sunshine." And he drives off. "Oh dear, I wish we could send Mummy away for a holiday," sighs Mr. Bear when they are indoors. "Only it costs a lot and we haven't enough money to pay for an extra holiday nowadays." "Never mind," says Rupert, "we'll do all her work for her and—look—I'll start by sweeping up this broken plate." Getting the brush and dustpan Rupert carefully collects the bits of the plate that Mrs. Bear broke and is just going to throw them away when a bright idea comes to him. "That plate was an odd one," he mutters, "but it was a favourite of Mummy's. If I could get another just like that it would make her happy!" Running to a cupboard he takes up his money-box and rattles it. "It's quite heavy. There may be enough there," he mutters.

RUPERT TAKES ALL HIS SAVINGS

"*There's just a chance I'll match this plate.*
I'd like to try, at any rate."

Then Rupert sets out, with new hope,
"*Don't rush,*" *smiles Daddy.* "*I can cope.*"

"*Try Pussyville for plates like that,*"
Says Pong-Ping, stopping for a chat.

"*Thanks,*" *smiles the little bear,* "*I will!*"
He hails the bus to Pussyville.

Mr. Bear has been busily preparing sandwiches to take to Mrs. Bear, but he pauses when Rupert runs forward carrying his money-box and the largest of the broken pieces of the plate and explains what he wants to do. "It's very generous of you to think of spending your savings in that way," Mr. Bear says. "I'm sure it would make Mummy very happy." Opening the box he gives Rupert the money and sees him set off to try to match the plate. Rupert has not gone very far when he realises that he does not know where he can buy a plate like the one his Mummy broke, so seeing more of his friends he tells them of his difficulty. "You won't get a nice plate of that colour in our village shop," says Pong-Ping the Peke, importantly. "You'd better try at Pussyville." Thanking his pals the little bear hurries away. "The bus will take me there," he thinks. "I can catch it at the crossroads." And he waits by the kerb until the Pussyville bus comes into sight.

RUPERT SEES LILY DUCKLING

In Pussyville, quite near the stop,
He finds a little china shop.

" The broken bit's a lovely shade,
But I can't match it, I'm afraid."

The little bear walks sadly out,
Then Lily Duckling gives a shout.

"Plates of this shade are very old,"
Sighs Rupert. " They're no longer sold."

The bus conductor tells Rupert when he has reached the middle of Pussyville and soon the little bear is trotting along and keeping a sharp look-out for the right shop. "Ah, here's one that sells cups and saucers. I'll try there," he thinks. The shopkeeper takes the broken fragment from him and looks at it curiously. Then she shakes her head sadly. "It's a lovely colour," she says, "but I don't think you'll find it again except, perhaps, in a very old plate. I have nothing like it in my shop." Rupert feels rather discouraged and, thanking the shop-lady, he walks out wondering what he should do next. Almost at once there is a patter of footsteps and who should appear but his friend Lily Duckling. "Hello, you here too!" he exclaims. "Yes, I often come here," Lily smiles. "I like looking at the shops and I like the bus ride. But what are you doing here?" Rupert rapidly tells her why he has come and asks if she can think of any way to help him.

RUPERT VISITS AN OLD SHOP

"Well, that shop sells old curios,
They might have some old plates, who knows?"

Into the window Rupert stares,
"They do sell plates here," he declares.

"Give me that fragment, little bear,
I've something of this shade! Now, where?"

"Please look, is this it?" Rupert cries.
"Yes," laughs the man. "Bless your sharp eyes."

Lily Duckling thinks quickly. "Yes, perhaps I can help," she quacks. "Your shop-lady said that the colour was only found in old plates. That means you don't want an ordinary china shop. I know this village well. There's an old curiosity shop over there. Why not try it?" "That's a topping idea!" cries Rupert, scampering away. "Yes, this does look a more likely place," he murmurs, "and there are even some plates there, though they are not quite like the one that Mummy broke." The old Curiosity Man invites Rupert into the shop and peers closely at the broken fragment. "I believe I've got something of that shade," he murmurs. "Now where is it?" Crossing to another wall he opens a showcase. All at once Rupert, who has been gazing at the quaint things in the shop, cries out: "Please, look, here's a plate of nearly the same colour." "Why, bless your sharp eyes, so it is!" laughs the man. "I've kept it for ages and nobody has wanted it, so you may have it cheap."

RUPERT BUYS THE PRESENT

"*It took up space I'd rather keep
For pictures, so I'll make it cheap.*"

"*Oh, thank you! You are very kind!*"
And Rupert hugs the well-wrapped find.

*He scuttles from the shop, and then
He almost bumps two gentlemen.*

"*I found a fine plate, thanks to you!
Mummy's favourite colour, too!*"

Rupert is delighted when he learns the price of the plate. "I can pay for that out of what was in my money-box," he smiles. "Mummy is sure to be happier when she sees it." When the old man hears why the little bear is so anxious to have the plate he becomes very friendly. "I must put in plenty of padding and pack it carefully in case you drop it on the way back," he says. Then he offers to show him other curiosities, but Rupert thanks him and says he must hurry home to cheer up his Mummy. As he scuttles out of the shop Rupert nearly bumps into two gentlemen who are striding briskly towards the doorway. They pay no attention to him, but Rupert glances with interest at the older man. "He looks important," he thinks, "but he is speaking in a strange way. I wonder where he comes from." However, he doesn't wait. Across the village green he spies Lily Duckling at the bus-stop and he runs to thank her for telling him of the shop and to tell her of his successful search.

RUPERT WATCHES TWO MEN

" Those men are coming over here,
They'll never catch this bus, I fear!"

" They seemed to shout at me! How strange!
Then waved, till we were out of range."

" Why, that's marvellous!" Daddy beams,
" The very shade, and how it gleams!"

The plate makes Mummy look so pleased,
At once she says she feels more eased.

Rupert finds that Lily Duckling too is ready to go home, and they do not have long to wait before the bus arrives. As they are getting on Rupert points. "Look, there are two men who were heading for that shop," he says. "They're hurrying. I wonder if they want to catch this bus." The conductor is upstairs and doesn't notice, so next minute they are moving off. "That older man is shouting and waving his arms," says Rupert, looking back. "It's strange, but I believe he's shouting at me!" After leaving the bus Rupert holds the parcel with the greatest care until he reaches his cottage and can unpack it in triumph to show the plate to his Daddy. "I say, that's marvellous," exclaims Mr. Bear. "Fancy you finding one of that colour so soon! I'll cut sandwiches for you to take to Mummy on it." Mrs. Bear is sitting up in a chair and Rupert has the joy of seeing her surprised and happy smile when she notices the plate and hears how he found it.

Rupert and the Broken Plate

RUPERT PUTS ON AN APRON

The story told, work starts again,
"I need an apron, it is plain!"

"I'll wash, you dry," says Mr. Bear,
"Here comes your new plate! Do take care!"

A sharp "rat-tat!" makes Rupert gasp,
The precious plate slips from his grasp.

"What bad luck!" Mr. Bear looks shocked,
He goes to find out who has knocked.

Mrs. Bear gets so cheerful when she realises that the breakage has been so well replaced that she speaks of starting her work again, but Rupert and his Daddy will not hear of it. "I think I could be jolly good at housework if you'd let me try," Rupert laughs. "Then you must be properly dressed for it," says Mrs. Bear. And she tells him in which drawer to find a little apron, and soon Rupert and his Daddy are busy washing up. "Here's your new plate," says Mr. Bear. "Be careful of it." Rupert stretches out his hand to take the plate from his Daddy. At that very moment a loud rat-tat-tat rings through the cottage and he is so startled at the suddenness of it that the precious plate slips through his fingers and with a crash it is shattered on the floor. They both gaze in horror at the pieces. "Oh, Rupert, what awful bad luck!" says his Daddy. "I can't help you for a minute. That knocking was at the front door. I must hurry along to see who it can be."

RUPERT FEELS VERY UPSET

Sobs Rupert, "Oh, what have I done?
I'll never find another one!"

"Two strangers want you! Come outside,"
Says Daddy, looking mystified.

"Why, it's those men who missed the bus!
Whatever do they want with us?"

Rupert is greeted with a bow,
"Ze little bear! We find 'im now!"

Scarcely able to believe the thing that has happened Rupert picks up one of the pieces of his latest plate. "Oh, this is too awful!" he sobs. "Just when I'd shown it to Mummy and made her happy. I could never have the luck to find another like it. And, even if I did, I've nothing left in my money-box to buy it with! What shall I do?" Then Mr. Bear returns, looking puzzled. "There are two strangers at the door, Rupert," he says. "They don't want me and they don't want Mummy. As far as I can make out they seem to want you!" Pausing to put down his apron Rupert follows to the front door and finds his Daddy talking to the strangers. "Hello, I've seen that coat before," he murmurs. "These are the men who were at the Pussyville shop. What brings them here?" As he advances the older man greets him briskly and politely. "Ah, it is 'im! Good day, little bear," he cries. "How lucky we are! We 'ave search and search and now we find. We 'ave ze luck, eh?"

RUPERT MEETS THE STRANGERS

"We seek some plates, owned long ago
By his own family, you know."

"He thinks the plate you bought may be
The last of them. Please, may we see?"

Though told the plate has just been smashed,
The strangers' hopes seem far from dashed.

"Ze pieces? You still 'ave zem, yes?"
The elder cries, in eagerness.

Seeing how puzzled Rupert looks the younger man bends down to explain. "I'm helping this other gentleman," he says. "He's from abroad and he has been searching for some old china that used to belong to his family. We traced the very last plate to England and we think you bought it just before we reached the Pussyville shop. Would you be so kind as to allow us to see it?" Rupert glances dolefully at his Daddy and Mr. Bear has to tell them that the plate has just been smashed. After the sad news that the plate has been broken Rupert expects the men to be angry or disappointed, or to go away, but to his surprise they only talk together quietly in a foreign language. In a very little while they nod at each other as though agreeing on something and when the elder gentleman comes forward he is actually smiling. "Ze break, it is nothing, it no mattaire," he says. "Ze bits, you 'ave zem, yes?" "Goodness, I do believe he wants the broken pieces," thinks Rupert in astonishment.

RUPERT GASPS AT THE STORY

"You not yet put zem in ze bin?
Ah, good!" He follows Rupert in.

He gazes at the lovely hue,
And at the broken edges too.

Then down the path the stranger stalks,
He waves a piece, and laughs and talks.

"He offers two pounds for the lot,
Whether they're what he thinks or not!"

What the two men want is quite clear, so Rupert turns back to enter the cottage. "Keep as quiet as you can," says Mr. Bear. "Mummy may hear us and worry." The men are too interested to wait in the garden, and are hard on Rupert's heels as he enters the kitchen. He sees them stare in excitement at the colour of the plate, but after a minute, to his surprise, they concentrate their attention on the jagged edges of the broken pieces. The elder gentleman suddenly strides out of the cottage, and

Mr. Bear and Rupert see him on the garden path waving one of the broken pieces and talking rapidly. Very soon the younger man returns and faces Rupert quietly. "My friend is nearly sure that he has found what he wants," he says. "He offers you two pounds for those pieces now, and a lot more later if they are what he thinks." "But I didn't give anything like that for the whole plate!" gasps Rupert. "I got it quite cheaply. The shopman said nobody wanted it!"

RUPERT GATHERS EVERY BIT

*"Take two pounds now, but you'll collect
Much more, if he is proved correct."*

*"This is beyond me! How on earth
Can broken bits have so much worth?"*

*"You've brought a hammer, Daddy! Why?"
Asks Rupert, but there's no reply.*

*It's clear the elder man now means
To smash the bits to smithereens!*

Rupert is taken aback by the generous offer, and cannot understand it. While he is hesitating the elder man comes in and waits anxiously to see what he will decide. "You'd better accept the money," says Mr. Bear. "We can put it in your money-box." "And remember, we shall want every one of those pieces," says the younger man. "This is beyond me," thinks Rupert as he picks up all the broken bits. "Why are these little pieces worth more now than the plate was before I smashed it?" Wrapping all the broken pieces in paper, Rupert returns to the group. "What have you brought that hammer for, Daddy?" he asks. There is no answer. Instead, the elder gentleman spreads the broken fragments on a table, seizes the hammer himself, and with a look of comical excitement he attacks them, cracking them into tinier and still tinier pieces. "Oh, please stop!" cries Rupert. "What are you doing? You've just paid me two pounds for those!" But the man only chuckles and continues.

RUPERT HAS A FINE REWARD

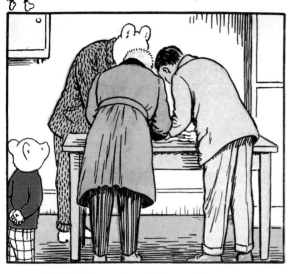

*Thinks Rupert Bear, "By now he must
Have hammered that poor plate to dust."*

*Then from the china dust are brought
The dazzling diamonds he sought!*

*"Some plates were made a special way,
Hiding the diamonds in the clay."*

*Now Rupert gets a grand reward!
He led them to the precious hoard.*

As the fragments of the plate are broken into very small pieces the three grown-ups bend more closely over the table so that Rupert cannot see what is going on. The hammering keeps on, though more gently. "That poor plate must be powder by now," mutters Rupert. All at once the elder man backs away and sits down, almost speechless with delight. In his hands is a dish covered with glittering stones. "Oo-oo, were those in the plate?" gasps Rupert. "They look like diamonds." When the precious stones are safely pocketed in a leather bag the younger man explains the mystery. "My friend comes from a wealthy family abroad," he says, "but long ago, during the bad times, one of his ancestors, wishing to conceal his treasure, had some plates made with the family diamonds hidden in the thickness of the china. We have now traced this, the last of the plates, and my friend wishes to give a reward." And Rupert finds himself clutching a bundle of notes which he shows Mr. Bear.

RUPERT SHOWS THE MONEY

"It's almost too much to receive!"
Gasps Rupert, as they take their leave.

"Oh, Mummy, such exciting news!
A holiday is yours to choose!"

"A sunny place will make you fit,
The Doctor was quite sure of it!"

"Who would believe one plate that broke
Could bring such happiness to folk!"

Rupert does not think it right to get so much money for nothing, but the strange gentleman insists with many smiles and much happy talk, of which the little bear cannot understand a word. Soon, waving his hat and his stick and the leather bag, he takes his leave. Rupert is quite bewildered. Then he rushes indoors. "I heard the sound of strangers," says Mrs. Bear. "Who were they? And where have you got all that money from?" And Rupert, full of excitement, tries to tell her every-thing at once. Mrs. Bear counts the big bundle of notes in astonishment. Then Mr. Bear comes in. "Your money-box is hardly big enough for all that," he says. "No, and I don't want to put it in my money-box," cries Rupert. "There should be enough here to send Mummy to a warm country so that she can get better quickly as Dr. Lion said. And if there's any over I'll give some to that kind shopman at Pussyville who let me have the plate cheap. And then we'll all be happy!"

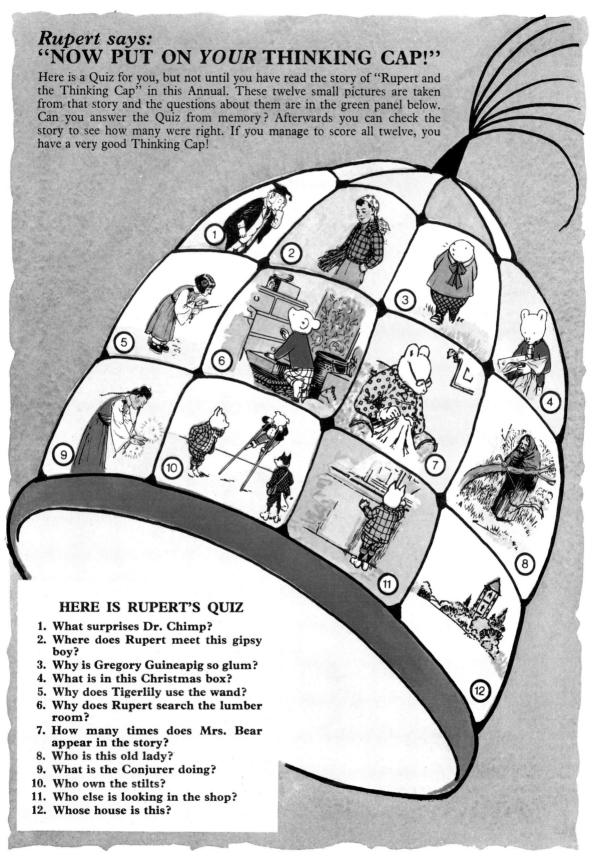

Rupert says:
"NOW PUT ON *YOUR* THINKING CAP!"

Here is a Quiz for you, but not until you have read the story of "Rupert and the Thinking Cap" in this Annual. These twelve small pictures are taken from that story and the questions about them are in the green panel below. Can you answer the Quiz from memory? Afterwards you can check the story to see how many were right. If you manage to score all twelve, you have a very good Thinking Cap!

HERE IS RUPERT'S QUIZ

1. What surprises Dr. Chimp?
2. Where does Rupert meet this gipsy boy?
3. Why is Gregory Guineapig so glum?
4. What is in this Christmas box?
5. Why does Tigerlily use the wand?
6. Why does Rupert search the lumber room?
7. How many times does Mrs. Bear appear in the story?
8. Who is this old lady?
9. What is the Conjurer doing?
10. Who own the stilts?
11. Who else is looking in the shop?
12. Whose house is this?

RUPERT and

RUPERT IS OFF TO THE SEASIDE

"Hi, Sailor Sam! We're just away,
Off to the seaside for the day."

"We'll bring a present back for you,"
Smiles Rupert, "as you can't come too."

MR. BEAR has borrowed an old car and has decided to take the family and Rupert's pal Bill Badger for a day at the sea. "It's jolly kind of you to invite me," says Bill, as Rupert carries the picnic things to the car. "We always have fun together, don't we?" "Rather!" laughs Rupert. "There was a spare seat, so Daddy let me choose who should go with us." Just as they are about to start their journey a familiar figure comes striding across the open ground. "It's Sailor Sam," says Rupert. "Hello, Sam. We're off to the seaside. Isn't it exciting!" "You lucky people! What part of the seaside?" asks Sam. "I don't know yet," replies Mr. Bear. "I'll go on until it looks interesting. Then I'll stop." "Oh dear, how I envy you!" says Sam. "I haven't been to the sea for ages." "Cheer up! We'll remember to bring you a present," smiles Rupert.

he BLUE STAR

Rupert and Bill find two of the creatures at the seaside. There are many more, and Sailor Sam knows they are a sign that he is threatened by a band of pirates. It is the start of a big adventure and Rupert has a part to play against Sam's enemies.

RUPERT'S DADDY STOPS HIS CAR

Sam waves goodbye. "That would be kind,
No sharks or whales or swordfish, mind!"

"We'll have our picnic on the shore,"
Says Mummy. "Then you can explore."

Rupert asks Sam what he would like as a present from the seaside, and the sailor grins broadly. "*Not* an octopus or a shark or a sea-serpent," he says. "They'd be too big for me to keep in my tiny shack. Just bring anything interesting to remind me of the briny and the days when I used to go on long voyages." He waves goodbye and off goes the little car. Mr. Bear does not hurry but drives steadily through the quiet lanes, and after a long journey they spy the sea and pull up on a grassy verge. Bill is the first to jump out and, running towards the cliffs, he turns and beckons the others. "We're in luck!" he shouts. "Here's a grand stretch of coast and nobody about." "Then we'll choose a picnic spot on the shore," Mrs. Bear decides, "and you two can go exploring." "Don't go far," chimes in Mr. Bear. "We can't stay more than an hour or two."

RUPERT AND BILL GO EXPLORING

Along the cliffs the two pals rove,
"Look! There's a ship moored in that cove!"

They clamber down. "This gully's steep!
And here's a cave! Bill, come and peep!"

Each scrambles through the narrow space,
Says Bill, "What an exciting place!"

"A starfish, Bill—a blue one, see!
Now that is something new to me!"

The little party has its picnic near the sea and then Rupert and Bill climb to the top of the cliffs. "Hi, look there," cries Bill. "D'you see those masts appearing over the edge? There must be a ship in that cove. I wish we could reach it." "I'm afraid we can't," says Rupert. "We promised not to go far, but I do wish I knew what ship it is." They decide to go down towards the sea by a rough gully and find it very steep. All at once Rupert notices a wide crack in the side of the gully. "I don't believe we can get down the rocks to the shore," he says. "This dark hole looks exciting. Shall we see where it leads?" Bill is always keen for something new and soon the two pals have squeezed into a gloomy cave below. "There's light beyond," says Bill. "There must be another way out." "Hey, what's this on the floor?" says Rupert. "It's a little sack. And look what's fallen out of it. Surely it's a starfish. But what a funny colour for a starfish. It's *blue*!"

RUPERT SOON SENSES DANGER

Then crunching footsteps make them shrink!
Breathes Bill, "They're coming here, I think!"

They hear gruff voices and a cough,
"Quick," whispers Rupert, "let's be off!"

"Those men sound rough, we mustn't stop!
Let's make our way up to the top."

"I'm glad we gave those men the slip,
Perhaps they came here on that ship."

Rupert stares at the curious thing on the rough floor. "*Is* it a starfish?" he says. "I've never heard of a *blue* one." He bends down, but before he can touch it there is a hiss from Bill. "Be quiet! There's someone coming!" he whispers urgently. Sure enough, there are gruff voices and the noise of footsteps crunching on pebbles. "I don't like the sound of those men," breathes Rupert. "Let's be off." And, as quietly as they can, they climb back towards the gap in the cliff.

Out in the open air the two friends retrieve their spades and pails. "We'll never reach the shore down that steep gully," says Rupert. "Let's go up again and return the way we came over the cliff-top." Once they are on the grass Bill looks wistfully towards the three masts. "I wish we could see it nearer," he murmurs. "I love ships." "Come on," urges Rupert. "It may belong to those men whose voices we didn't like. Besides, Daddy doesn't want us to be away too long."

RUPERT SUDDENLY TOPPLES

The pals run on, until they reach
An easy pathway to the beach.

A starfish glistens in the sun,
"It's blue! Just like that other one!"

The thing glows with a bluish light,
One touch, and Rupert jumps in fright!

A violent shock runs up his arm,
He cringes back in great alarm.

When they are halfway back the two pals pause again. "That way down looks much easier than the gully," says Rupert. "The tide's going out, so we should be able to work round the headland and join Mummy and Daddy at their picnic point." This time they succeed, and make their different way among the rocks and pools of the upper shore. All at once Rupert, who has been faster than Bill, stares at something as if he can hardly believe what he sees lying on the sand among the rocks. What

has startled Rupert is a small object lying between some boulders, an object with five points. "It's another starfish. Another *blue* one!" he mutters. Going to it he bends down to pick it up. Then he topples back in fright for barely has he touched it when the points curl up and a violent shock runs up his arm. Lifting himself up, he gives a shout just as his pal comes to join him. "Whatever's up now?" Bill demands. "Have you had a tumble or lost something? What are you staring at?"

RUPERT WARNS HIS FRIEND

*"It's still alive, Bill, leave it be!
It's full of electricity!"*

*Too late! Bill leaps back, "Oh, my hat!
It's foreign! Ours don't shock like that!"*

*"It's high and dry!" They stare in awe,
"Perhaps it's from that sack we saw."*

*The chums recover in a while,
Says Rupert, "This will make Sam smile!"*

Moving forward Bill Badger notices the strange thing lying on the shingle. "What, another *blue* starfish!" he exclaims. "Where do they come from? Is it alive?" "Yes, yes it is," cries Rupert. "Let it alone. It's dangerous!" But Bill has already touched it, and he leaps back with a scared look as the starfish does its trick again. "W-what is it?" he says, shakily. "Is it a real one?" When the two pals feel better after their shocks they stand and gaze at the blue starfish. "I don't under-stand how it got here," says Bill, as an idea strikes him. "It's still alive, but the sea didn't bring it here. The tide's just going out and didn't come up quite as high as this." "I wonder if it was dropped from that sack we saw in the cave," says Rupert. "I tell you what—it's just the sort of thing that would interest Sailor Sam. Let's take it back." And very gingerly he carries his pail nearer and picks up the strange blue starfish on his wooden spade.

RUPERT DROPS THE BUCKET

They fill the bucket from a pool,
"It wants salt water, nice and cool."

"Oo!-Ow! The pail's electric now!
I cannot hold it anyhow!"

With wooden spades to guard their hands,
They bring the pail across the sands.

"Blue starfish? Gives electric shocks?"
Gasps Daddy. "Stranded near the rocks?"

The starfish lies quietly in the pail, and Rupert starts to carry it away. "It's making my arm feel funny," he grins. "That thing must still be alive!" "Perhaps the poor thing wants some salt water," says Bill. So they stop at the nearest pool and Bill uses the other bucket to pour in water. "Now it'll be heavier," says Rupert. "I'll carry it first and—Oo!—Ow!—Eee!—I c-c-can't! The whole bucket's electric now. I'm tingling all over!" And, in alarm, he drops both his spade and bucket

hurriedly. Meanwhile, Mrs. Bear is packing up the picnic things. "Rupert and Bill have been away a long time," she says. "I hope they are safe." "See, here they come," says Mr. Bear. "They're carrying something." "Look, Daddy, a new starfish," says Rupert when he arrives. "It's blue, and it made the pail too electric to hold, but we found that when we put the wooden spades through the handle we could carry it." Mr. Bear stares and murmurs: "My, the things you do find."

RUPERT CAN'T KEEP HIS FIND

"We'll take the starfish back for Sam,"
Says Rupert. "Mind the doors don't slam!"

"The engine won't start! Get outside!
The whole car's gone electrified!"

"It's that blue starfish, I'm afraid,
Remove it! Use a wooden spade!"

"Let's find a pool where it can live!
Poor Sam, we've nothing else to give!"

Mr. and Mrs. Bear tell the little pals to leave the blue starfish as it is time to go home. "Oh, *please,* can't we take it with us?" pleads Rupert. "We promised Sailor Sam that we'd bring him something, and we've seen nothing as interesting as this!" So Mr. Bear gives them a large handkerchief to tie over the pail. They all get in, and he tries to start the engine. "Here, what on earth's happening?" he gasps. For the whole car is now quivering and tingling. So is everyone in it! The engine splutters and wheezes, but will not start, so they all get out. "The thing you put in there must be causing the trouble," says Mr. Bear. "It must go or we shall never get home." "The pail is as hard to catch hold of as it was before," says Rupert, as he touches it. "Let's put the wooden spade through the handle again." They do so and are soon able to return to the shore. "I wish I knew how this thing managed to be such a nuisance," says Bill with a frown.

RUPERT GETS HOME AT DUSK

They tip it in. "I only wish
Sam could have seen you, Blue Starfish!"

Soon they are in the car again,
And speeding homeward, right as rain.

"Let's call on Sam tomorrow, Bill!
Our tale should give him quite a thrill."

Next morning Rupert waits alone,
"Bill's late! I'll set off on my own."

"I wish things hadn't turned out quite like this," murmurs Rupert. "I did want to take something interesting back to Sailor Sam, and this blue starfish is the oddest thing we've seen today. I expect it needs salt water to keep it alive. Look, here's a pool left at the very top of the tide." They put the pail at the edge of the pool, and Rupert gently tips the creature out. Soon they are in the car again. "Good, there's nothing wrong with the engine now," says Mr. Bear as he drives briskly away. So much time has been wasted because of the unexpected behaviour of the starfish that evening has nearly closed in before Mr. Bear brings the hired car safely home. "Join me again tomorrow, Bill," says Rupert. "You must help me tell Sailor Sam all about what we saw at the seaside." "Right-o, I'll come," says Bill. "I must hurry now, my Daddy will think I'm lost." And next morning Rupert looks out for him eagerly. When Bill does not appear he becomes impatient.

RUPERT'S TALE ALARMS SAM

He dashes off without his chum,
"Ahoy!" calls Sam. "I'm glad you've come."

Laughs Rupert, "Sam, we nearly brought
A strange blue starfish that we caught!"

"You saw some ship's masts? Then you found
A blue star . . . What?" Sam whirls around.

"The Blue Star? Are you sure of this?
Then something's very much amiss!"

Bill does not turn up at the expected time and Rupert asks Mrs. Bear if he may go alone to see his friend Sailor Sam. "When Bill comes, please tell him that I'm ahead of him," he says as he sets off. Sailor Sam is in the garden of his shack when he arrives. "Well, little bear, did you have a good day at the sea?" smiles the sailor. "Did you bring me a present?" "Not quite," laughs Rupert. "But you'd be surprised at what we nearly brought!" And he tells his friend of all that happened when the blue starfish was put in the car. Sailor Sam walks towards his shack while Rupert is talking. "I expect you'd like some lemonade and a biscuit," he smiles. "What a nice day you had. So you saw the masts of a sailing ship and then found a starfish . . ." He pauses suddenly and swings round. "What did you say? A blue one?" Going inside he sits down abruptly and stares at the little bear. "It can't be, it can't be true!" he breathes. "The *Blue Star?* Are you sure?"

RUPERT LEARNS OF AN ISLAND

"It comes," cries Sam, a map unfurled,
"From just one island in the world!"

"It didn't swim this far, or fly!
So someone shipped it here! But why?"

"Black Pedro brought them! Now I guess,
To put me out of action, yes!"

"He wants this box! Aye, that's his plan!
Twas left me by a sailor man."

Rupert is astonished at his friend's excitement. "Is the blue starfish very rare?" he asks. "*Rare!* Of course it's rare!" exclaims Sam. "It only lives in one place in the world." He unrolls the map of an island. "There, that's one of Cap'n Morgan's smuggling haunts," he says. "It's far, far away and the Blue Star lives there. It could never have travelled all this way alone over the bed of the sea. That means that somebody has troubled to bring Blue Stars here." Rupert tries hard to understand.

"But why shouldn't people bring them?" he asks. "Because they're terrible, dangerous, and poisonous," says Sam. "You're lucky you only got an electric shock. If you had a scratch from one of its thousands of little spikes you might have been very ill. Now who can have brought that sack full of them?" All of a sudden he gives a gasp. "Tis Black Pedro!" he shouts. "It can be no other! Wait, I'll show you." And he produces a little iron box from its hiding place.

RUPERT SHARES A BIG SECRET

Upon a paper, old and brown,
Some foreign words are written down.

"Its meaning, some wise man must tell,
Till then," says Sam, "I'll guard it well."

"'Tis my belief, it tells," he sighs,
"Where some great hidden treasure lies."

A rustle's heard outside the door,
"Why, here's a parcel! Who's it for?"

Rupert is now quite bewildered. "Black Pedro? Who is Black Pedro?" he asks. "He's my only real enemy," says Sailor Sam gloomily. "He knows Cap'n Morgan's island where the Blue Stars can be found. And I believe that he has found out that I've got this. Look." And from the heavy little box he produces a piece of old, tough brown paper. "There's writing on it," says Rupert, "but I don't understand a word of it." "No wonder," says Sam. "Neither can I! I don't know that lingo." Sam ponders over the faded paper. "The box was left me by an old sailor man who used to be a smuggler himself," he says. "This paper was the only thing in it and it's my belief that it tells the secret of a great hidden treasure. If so, it's very, very precious and must be guarded until some clever person tells me its meaning." Then Rupert hears a little sound and he goes to the door. Outside there is no one in sight, but lying close to the doorstep is a small package with a label tied to it.

RUPERT MUST STAND AWAY

"For you, Sam! There's a label on,
Whoever left it here has gone."

Suspiciously, Sam opens it,
"I'll tip it out, stand back a bit."

"Don't touch! A Blue Star! Keep your head,
It's dangerous, although it's dead!"

"It's from Black Pedro! I must act!
He means to harm me, it's a fact!"

Sailor Sam has followed Rupert to the door. "Look here," says the little bear. "This parcel is addressed to you. It wasn't there when we came in. Perhaps it is meant as a surprise. Is it your birthday?" "No, it isn't! And I don't like people leaving parcels and then sneaking away," says Sam, who is already in a very nervous state. "Let me have it." He takes it gingerly and unfastens the paper with the greatest care. Then he flicks off the lid. Inside the box is tissue paper and, instead of undoing it, Sam tips it out on the table. Immediately he waves Rupert back. "Don't touch!" he shouts. "Look what it is! A Blue Star. It's a dead one, but just as dangerous! Just what I thought, this must be from Black Pedro, who wants to put me out of action. I must have help. Who can I get? Constable Growler is the nearest. Oh dear, I must go." He is so agitated that he dashes straight out, forgetting that he has left Rupert alone at the shack.

RUPERT STAYS IN THE SHACK

"The Constable's the one I need!"
Sam rushes off at frantic speed.

"Sam's paper! I must put it back!"
Thinks Rupert, trembling, in the shack.

He lifts the box, a heavy thing,
Then—snap!—the lid shuts, on a spring.

"Sam took the key! The lid's tight shut!
What's that? Who's coming to the hut?"

·Things have been happening too fast for poor Rupert since arriving at Sailor Sam's shack, and the sudden departure of his friend leaves him stranded and rather frightened. "What had I better do?" he thinks, as he goes into the shack again. "I mustn't touch that awful blue starfish. And, oh goodness me! Sam's forgotten to put away that precious old paper. Suppose anyone comes. That's the one thing he will be anxious not to lose. The best thing I can do, I suppose, is to see to it for him." Rupert looks at the little iron box. "I wonder if I can find the place where he hides that," he murmurs, "and whether it is too heavy for him to carry." He tugs it off the table, but just as he gets it into his arms the lid closes with a snap. "Oh dear, I must open it to put the old paper in," he thinks. "I didn't know the lid was on a spring. And now it won't open again! And Sam's taken the key." All at once he stops to listen. "What was that noise?" he whispers.

RUPERT FACES A GRIM FIGURE

Thinks Rupert, "Good, my jersey's tight,"
He stuffs the paper out of sight.

He's just in time! The door bursts wide,
A grim-faced stranger steps inside.

He sweeps aside the little bear,
Then spies the box, still lying there.

"That's it! The smuggler's box!" he grins.
"And now 'tis mine! The best man wins!"

The noise that Rupert has heard comes nearer. "There's somebody outside," he thinks. "That is not Sam's footstep. Who can it be?" Though he pulls feverishly at the lid of the iron box it will not open. At last he grabs the precious old paper and stuffs it under his jersey. He is just in time to straighten up as the door bursts open and a grim figure in strange clothes strides in. "And who are you?" growls the man. "I thought the sailor lived alone." Rupert is startled and scared by the stranger's sudden appearance. "Oh p-please, I'm a friend of Sam's," he quavers. "And I called to see him because he asked for something from the seaside and . . ." But the other does not seem to be listening. Still frowning he peers keenly around. He looks without surprise at the dead starfish, then rushes towards the iron box. "That's it, that's it!" he hisses. "Tis the very thing I came for! Cap'n Morgan's carpenter, Old Jem, owned that box. Many's the time I've seen it. Now 'tis mine!"

RUPERT IS SEIZED BY THE MAN

"That box is Sam's! You leave it here!
He'll bring the policeman, never fear!"

"Black Pedro can't be caught by such!
You come with me! You talk too much."

"Black Pedro!" Rupert thinks, in dread,
As through deep woodland he is sped.

A hard man, waiting in a glade,
Points at a shelter, roughly made.

As the man seizes the black box and tucks it under his arm Rupert screws up his courage to speak. "Put that down!" he says, trembling. "It belongs to Sailor Sam, and he's gone to fetch Constable Growler. He'll be back any minute." "Oh, will he?" The man seems amused at something. "I think not, little bear. Black Pedro cannot be caught by simple sailors or country coppers! Nor will he leave *you* here to give the alarm. You come with me." And grabbing Rupert, he marches

him rapidly out of the shack. The man, holding Rupert firmly, urges him into the nearby woods. The little bear is very scared at what he has heard. "He spoke of Black Pedro," he thinks. "Can he himself be Black Pedro? That's the name of Sailor Sam's enemy. Oh, I do hope that Sam will hurry up and bring help." On they go until they reach a rough shelter of branches covered with foliage. Then a fierce-looking man appears and, pointing at the shelter, he says some foreign words.

RUPERT HAS NO WAY OF ESCAPE

" *Yes, it's the very box, at last!*
We need the key, so search him fast! "

The man comes back. " *No key!* " *he moans.*
" *Now how we open box?* " *he groans.*

" *We'll break it open later on,*
Now tie him up, and let's be gone! "

Into the shelter Rupert's borne,
And left there, frightened and forlorn.

The newcomer catches sight of the black box under Pedro's arm and becomes suddenly excited. Pedro grins darkly. "Yes, it's the very box," he says. "The key was not in it but no matter. Search him quickly and get it." The other man dives into the shelter and Rupert hears noises inside. "What does it mean?" he thinks. "Who is being searched?" In a few minutes the man appears again, looking angry. "No good, no key, no not'ing," he whines. "Him pockets empty."

Black Pedro is very annoyed at what his man has said. "We must not wait for more," he growls. "A cold chisel must serve our purpose as there is no key. Now to get away. But we must not leave that little creature to tell his story until we are well clear. Truss him up and put him out of sight." And while the other men gather round, Rupert finds his wrists and ankles tied and his arms bound tightly. Then he is lifted and carried into the semi-darkness of the shelter and dumped on his back.

RUPERT AND SAM ARE CAPTIVES

The men run off and disappear,
Then he hears muffled sounds, quite near.

He shuffles forward on his knees,
"A pair of boots! Who is it, please?"

"Oh Sam, what have they done to you?"
Gasps Rupert. "Now what shall we do?"

He turns abruptly, on his guard,
"Who called my name?" He listens hard.

Rupert listens to the gruff voices of Black Pedro and his crew, first arguing and then becoming fainter, and by squirming over he manages to sit up in time to see the men disappearing downhill. While he is wondering what he can do to get free from the ropes he hears another sound, muffled and much nearer. "There's somebody else here," he breathes. After more squirming he is able to kneel up and peer into the darkness of the shelter. "Surely I can see a pair of boots!" he whispers.

"There *is* someone here!" Knowing that he is not alone, Rupert calls into the darkness. The answer is a low grunt and a straining noise. Rupert contrives to shuffle forward and to his astonishment, he makes out the figure of his friend Sailor Sam lying bound in the darkness with a cloth tied over his mouth. "Oh Sam, what have they done to you? How did they catch you?" he gasps. Suddenly he turns. "Listen!" he whispers urgently. "There, *another* voice. Somebody's calling my name!"

RUPERT IS QUICKLY SET FREE

"Why, Bill, it's you! How glad I am!
Quick, rescue me and Sailor Sam!"

"I saw you dragged away, and then
I followed, hiding in the glen."

Frowns Sam, "They trapped me as I left,
Then dumped me in this leafy cleft."

"Black Pedro came, your enemy!
He stole your black box! Where's the key?"

Rupert shouts in answer to the call and tries to shuffle back. Before he can reach the entrance a familiar figure hurries forward. "Oh Bill, Bill, I am glad to see you!" cries the little bear. "Where have you been?" "I had to run errands for my Mummy, so I couldn't join you when you went to see Sam," says Bill, "but I went later and saw you dragged away and I've followed, keeping out of sight. What does it all mean?" He rapidly unfastens Rupert's cords and listens to the strange story. When Rupert is free, he and Bill lose no time in undoing the cords on Sailor Sam's ankles and arms. "Those villains were waiting in ambush as I ran for Constable Growler," says Sam angrily. "They overpowered me, but why were *you* caught, little bear?" "Your enemy Black Pedro came to your shack," says Rupert. "He stole your heavy little black box and then he dragged me here in case I told anyone. Wasn't it wonderful luck that my pal Bill saw what happened?"

RUPERT LOOKS FOR THE ROGUES

Sighs Sam, "I dropped it on the way,
But he will force the lock, I'd say."

"They took the river path," says Bill.
"Let's follow! We may catch them still."

"Those rogues have given us the slip,"
Says Sam. "They're making for their ship!"

"The coastguards! They're the men to get!"
And Sam trots off, not beaten yet.

Sailor Sam stands up and looks quite baffled. "Those rogues are too clever," he moans. "But they did fail when they searched me for the key of the box. At the moment I was grabbed I managed to drop the key into the long grass without their seeing it, so that they should not get it. And what can we do now?" Rupert hesitates, but Bill speaks up. "I've been hiding and have watched what happened," he says. "Those men have gone towards the river." "Then let's keep them in sight," says Sam grimly. Going cautiously and listening to every sound, Sam leads the little pals downhill, and at length they reach the river. "Too late!" growls the sailor. "What terrible luck. They've got too much start of us. Oh, the rascals! They'll go back to their ship." "Can't we still tell Constable Growler?" asks Rupert nervously. "He might be able to alert the coastguards," says Sam. "It's our only chance." And, puffing with his efforts, he trots uphill again ahead of the chums.

RUPERT STILL HAS THE PAPER

But now his head begins to spin,
"Can't keep this up! I'm all done in!"

"They haven't won! That's where you're wrong!
The paper's been safe, all along!"

"I quite forgot in all this haste!"
And Rupert pulls it from his waist.

Sam seizes it in disbelief,
Then gazes, speechless with relief.

Near the top of the slope Sailor Sam sinks on to a boulder and mops his brow. "'Tis no use," he gasps breathlessly. "Can't keep up this sort of thing—too old for hurrying uphill—never could run much, anyway—oh, dear, oh, dear—iron box gone—Black Pedro gone, never catch him now—oh, dear." Suddenly Rupert gives a start. "No, no, you're wrong!" he shouts. "All this excitement made me forget what happened. Black Pedro has gone, and he has the iron box, but he *hasn't* got the old paper!" Sailor Sam stares at the little bear. "What d'you mean?" he demands. "How do you know? If Black Pedro hasn't got the ancient paper, where is it?" "It's here!" laughs Rupert. "I've got it myself! When I first heard Pedro coming I was scared. I didn't know where to hide the paper, so I stuffed it in the only place I could think of. See, here it is!" And from under his jersey he pulls the precious, faded sheet. Sam seizes it, and for some moments he cannot say a word.

RUPERT MAKES SAM CHEERFUL

Dancing a hornpipe in his joy,
He laughs, "My paper's safe! Ahoy!"

"I'd love to see Black Pedro's scowl!
That empty box will make him growl!"

"I've buried that dead starfish, true!
But we have one more job to do."

The chums race home across the green,
"Another task? What does Sam mean?"

When Sailor Sam realises that his main anxiety has so suddenly been removed he forgets how tired he is, and, waving the paper in the air, he dances a little hornpipe in his delight. "So it's not lost. It's not lost!" he laughs as he capers about. "This may make my fortune yet. Just think what we've done to Black Pedro. He's got the iron box without the key. How lovely! I'd give a lot to see his face when he chisels it open and finds it empty! Come on, Rupert! That was smart work!" Sailor Sam, now feeling as spry as ever, takes the little pals back to his shack. "That Blue Star is still on the table," he says. "It's dead, but it's as poisonous and dangerous as ever." Picking it up between two pieces of wood he carries it out to bury it. "And is that the end of the adventure?" asks Rupert. "Well, it's time you went home," says Sam, "but it's not the end by any means. I'll call for you tomorrow." "That sounds very mysterious," Rupert smiles as they scamper off.

RUPERT EXPECTS HIS FRIENDS

*"Oh Mummy, there's so much to tell!
Sam wants us both again, as well!"*

*Next morning Rupert gives a shout,
"Sam's here, with Bill!" He dashes out.*

*"Hello," grins Sam, "I thought you'd like
A trip on my old motor-bike."*

*"Could they ride in my sidecar, please?"
He asks, and Mrs. Bear agrees.*

Still wondering about Sailor Sam's latest words the two pals reach the Bears' cottage. "Oo, Mummy, we've had such a time!" says Rupert. "If it wasn't for Bill I shouldn't be here now. He's got to go to his home, but he'll be back tomorrow and Sailor Sam wants us both and . . ." "Here, here, not so fast," says Mrs. Bear. "You're very late. Come in and have your tea." And she listens to the strange story. Next morning, after breakfast, Rupert looks out. "Sam's here, just as he said he would be," he calls. Rupert finds Sailor Sam holding a mysterious contraption and securing all sorts of things to his old motor-bike and sidecar. "I picked up Bill to save time," says Sam. Just then Mrs. Bear bustles towards them. "What's all this?" she demands. "This affair with dangerous starfishes frightens me. Can't you leave Rupert alone now?" "No, Ma'am," says the sailor firmly. "It's because they're dangerous that I *do* need Rupert now. But I'll keep him quite safe."

RUPERT SPEEDS TO THE COAST

They set off, with a heavy load,
And drive along the coastal road.

Says Sam, " You came here? *Right you are!*
Now, guide me to that live Blue Star!"

" Yes, here's the pool! We've found the spot!
But is the Star still there, or not?"

Sam follows with a load of gear,
" One little test will make that clear."

Having persuaded Mrs. Bear to give her consent, Sailor Sam puts Rupert and Bill into his sidecar and the old motor-bike roars away. "This isn't very comfortable," says Bill as they bounce along. "What are we sitting on?" "Probably my gum-boots," shouts Sam above the din. "What a weird lot of stuff you're carrying," shouts Rupert. "Never mind about that," says Sam. "All I want you to do is to guide me to the spot where you left the live Blue Star." Rupert does so and they all descend to the rocks. Picking out their landmarks, Rupert and Bill find the spot where they put the starfish into the water. There is no sign of it now, but they call to Sailor Sam who hurries to them wearing his gum-boots and carrying a wooden pail, wooden-handled spade and his curious object with lots of hosepipe. "I expect you see my idea," he says. "You told me that you had left that Blue Star in the very highest pool left by the tide. The odds are that it's still there!"

RUPERT EMPTIES THE POOL

"Yes, yes! The pool's electric! Fine!
Let's use that stirrup pump of mine!"

"You take this hose-pipe," Rupert's told,
"It's rubber, and quite safe to hold."

Sam works the pump with all his strength,
"Right, that's enough!" he calls, at length.

"The live Blue Star! We'll take it home,
It's dangerous, and mustn't roam."

Rupert and Bill show Sam the exact spot where the starfish was tipped into the water, and the sailor dips his finger gingerly. Then he rises in great excitement. "The water's electric. The Star's still there!" he exclaims. Walking into the pool he stands his strange instrument in front of him. "This is what they call a stirrup pump," he says. "Your daddy will know what it's for. Will you take this hose and carry the end a little way off? It's rubber and won't make your fingers tingle." Rupert takes the end of the hosepipe away from the pool and beyond a boulder. "Point the nozzle well away from you," says Sailor Sam, "and don't get splashed with this electrified water. There's no wind, so it won't be blown back on to you." Then he works the pump vigorously and a jet of water appears. At length there is a cry from Sam and, dropping the hose, the two pals find him lifting the Blue Star from the nearly-empty pool, and putting it into the wooden bucket.

RUPERT AND BILL GO FIRST

"Now where's that sack of which you spoke?
Those dead Stars could cause harm to folk."

Back to the motor-bike they climb,
Says Sam, "We'll need a rope this time."

They find the gully, cave and all,
Sam squeezes in, then gives a call.

The sack of dead Blue Stars is found,
Then safely buried in the ground.

Rupert is delighted at the success of their work. "The Blue Star was there safe enough, hiding under a bit of seaweed," he grins. "I'll warrant it's the first one ever to be found alive in these parts," says Sailor Sam. He puts water in the pail and carries it to a safe place up on the cliff-top. "Now you must show me where your cave with the little sack of dead starfishes was," he says, and Rupert and Bill lead the way. "Those masts that we saw here yesterday have disappeared," says Bill. "They *must* have belonged to Black Pedro's ship!" Rupert and Bill show Sailor Sam the crack by which they reached the cave. "I'm a bit too big to get in there," murmurs Sam. However, he does manage it and takes a coil of rope with him. Later, he appears again. "The sack of Blue Stars was still there," he says. "I'll bury them at once, so there'll be no danger of them hurting other folk. Here they are, tied with my cord." He drops the sack and sets to work digging near some bushes.

RUPERT RUNS TO THE DWARF

"They're harmless now, and no mistake,
Let's go! We've one more call to make."

At length they stop, and cross a slope,
"The old Professor's in, I hope."

The servant looks up from his tasks,
"Rupert! What brings you here?" he asks.

"Professor!" cries the little bear,
"Sam's brought you something very rare!"

"Well, we really are getting on," grins Sam, as he ties a cloth over his bucket. "Now that electrified water can't splash you. We'll pack up and go. The dangerous part of the affair is over. Now for the interesting bit." "I wonder what he means," says Bill. On the return journey the sailor stops short of Nutwood and they all trot across a slope. "Why, that's the old Professor's house," says Rupert. "Is that where we're going?" Sailor Sam sends Rupert on ahead to see if anyone is at home, and almost at once the small figure of the Professor's servant appears in sight. "Hello, have you come to see my master?" says the kindly dwarf. "I'll call him." Soon they are all at the front door, and the Professor is welcoming them. "Come in, come in," he says genially. "I like Rupert to call. He always brings something interesting." "Well, it's not me this time," Rupert smiles. "It's Sailor Sam who has brought something interesting. It's in this bucket. May we show you?"

RUPERT LISTENS EXCITEDLY

"The Blue Star, Rupert! What a find!
I'll keep it, yes. You're very kind."

"The Star has found a safe retreat!"
Then Sam reveals the precious sheet.

Now, telling all that has occurred,
Sam sighs, "I can't translate one word."

"It's Sea-dog Spanish! We must look
In this old Spanish language book."

After peering into the wooden bucket the old Professor becomes very eager and, fetching a transparent plastic bowl, he helps Sam to tip the Blue Star into it. "Isn't it a horrid, poisonous thing?" says Rupert. But the old gentleman is gazing in delight. "This is going to be the pride of my collection," he gloats. "It shall have a tank to itself. Never did I expect to have anything so rare!" While he moves to make arrangements Sam quietly pulls something from the top of his jacket.

It is the precious faded paper that was the cause of the whole adventure, and now he tells the Professor of the escape they have had. "H'm, it must be more than usually important," says the old gentleman. "Let's see, what's it written in? It's no language that I know. I do believe that it's old Sea-Dog Spanish. We must look into this." Going into his library he takes down a small volume and studies the wording on the faded paper carefully. Gradually his face shows a satisfied smile.

RUPERT BEGS TO TAKE PART

"It tells where buried treasure lies,
On this far isle!" the old man cries.

"To think Black Pedro doesn't know!
That island is his lair! Ho-ho!"

The old man calls, "I wish you luck!
You'll find that treasure, you've got pluck!"

Pleads Rupert Bear, "You mustn't fail
To take me with you, when you sail!"

The old Professor checks and re-checks the words on the precious paper. Then he points to an island on one of the maps. "It's quite clear now," he says. "That paper tells of great treasure buried by a former pirate on the south-west coast of this island." "Well, of all things!" Sam laughs. "'Tis the very island where Black Pedro and his gang have their lair! They may be walking over the treasure every day and never knowing it!" The Professor is nearly as excited as Sailor Sam. "My,

my, I wish I was young enough to be with you when you sail away to find that treasure," he says, as the three visitors set out for home. Outside his own cottage Rupert turns eagerly. "Please, please will you take me with you when you go treasure-hunting?" he pleads. "Surely *I'm* young enough." Sailor Sam smiles happily. "We'll see when the time comes," he says. "I can't make promises yet, not while your Mummy is giving me one of her old-fashioned looks!"

ANOTHER ISLAND PUZZLE FOR RUPERT

When Sam finds another precious paper that used to belong to old Jem the carpenter, he gets very excited. "Look at this, Rupert!" he cries. "Here's a map of a sandy island that grows nothing but palm trees, and they all have numbers. Now we can go straight to where the treasure is buried!"

Why is Sam so sure? First read the story of the Blue Star, then follow the clues written on this map and see if you can spot the palm tree beside which the pirate captain's gold is buried. The answer to the puzzle is on page 115.

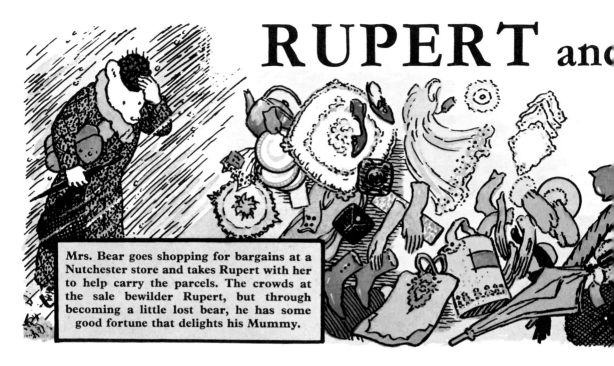

RUPERT and

Mrs. Bear goes shopping for bargains at a Nutchester store and takes Rupert with her to help carry the parcels. The crowds at the sale bewilder Rupert, but through becoming a little lost bear, he has some good fortune that delights his Mummy.

RUPERT SITS UP WITH A START

"What woke me?" Rupert starts and stares,
"It's much too early," he declares.

"Get dressed," says Daddy, with a yawn,
"Mummy was up at crack of dawn!"

RUPERT has been sound asleep when something makes him open his eyes and lift his head off the pillow. "I wonder what woke me up," he whispers. "It's not getting up time. Are Mummy and Daddy about yet?" Hearing a little sound in the passage, he slips out of bed and opens the door. He finds Daddy there in his dressing-gown, looking very sleepy. "Hallo, Daddy, what's going on?" says Rupert. "Is any-thing the matter?" "No, nothing's wrong," replies Mr. Bear with a yawn. "But Mummy's dressed already and is making us an early breakfast, though it's hardly seven o'clock. Oh dear, she does this once a year and I do wish she wouldn't. It's so chilly this time of morning. You'd better get yourself dressed too. Mummy won't be at all pleased if we keep her waiting." Daddy seems in no mood to explain, so Rupert does as he is told.

the WINTER SALE

RUPERT'S MUMMY BUSTLES ABOUT

Breakfast is hurried. "Do make haste,"
Calls Mummy, "I've no time to waste."

"I'm taking Rupert," Daddy's told,
"There'll be some parcels he can hold."

Breakfast is an odd meal today. Mrs. Bear finishes first and says very little, being busy jotting down notes on a piece of paper and murmuring to herself. Soon she is bustling into her outdoor clothes. "Now then, Daddy," she says briskly. "Mind you have the washing-up done when I get back. I've decided to take Rupert with me. He's good at carrying parcels." "If it's shopping you need from the village, Mummy," says Rupert, "I could do it for you. One of my chums could help——" "Dear me, it's far more important than that," interrupts Mrs. Bear. "We are spending the day at Nutchester. Do be quick, we mustn't miss the bus or we'll have an hour to wait." Mr. Bear looks up from his newspaper and chuckles as Mummy prepares to leave. "Poor Rupert," he says. "I feel so sorry for him. Are you going to buy him a suit of armour? He will need it!"

RUPERT TRAVELS ON THE BUS

"Your Mummy's on the warpath, yes!
You should be wearing battle-dress!"

"Come on," says Mummy, with a frown,
"We'll catch the early bus to town."

A queue has formed, they join the end,
Just then the bus comes round the bend.

"There'll be a fight to get first choice,"
Says Mummy, in a teasing voice.

Rupert hurries into his overcoat. "What do you mean about me having a suit of armour, Daddy?" he asks. "Well, your Mummy's on the warpath," smiles Mr. Bear. "She may need someone to protect her in the battle." "Tcha! Such nonsense!" says Mrs. Bear as she walks out. "Come on, Rupert." And, wondering what on earth his Daddy was talking about, Rupert trots along with her. "We're in time for the early bus," says Mrs. Bear. "There's Mrs. Badger." Mrs. Bear strides onward in a very determined way. "Look what a lot of others are coming here," says Rupert. "Why are all the ladies of the village catching this bus, Mummy?" "I expect they all have the same idea as I have," answers Mrs. Bear. Then the bus rumbles up and they all crowd in, talking brightly. "Shall we go together?" says Mrs. Badger. "We might help each other." "No, we might fight over something we want!" laughs Mrs. Bear. And Rupert is more mystified than ever.

RUPERT ARRIVES AT A STORE

At Nutchester they all climb out,
Breathes Rupert, "What's this all about?"

"We're nice and early, that's a boon,
The crowd will be much bigger soon."

A queue goes halfway round the store,
Gasps Rupert,"I can't see the door!"

Says Mummy, "See that lovely hat?
I've come here chiefly to buy that."

When the bus stops at Nutchester there is a general scramble to get out. "I don't believe there was a single man in the bus," says Rupert. "What a hurry all those ladies are in. Look, they're all going in the same direction. What's the excitement? Are we going to a cinema?" "No, not exactly," says Mrs. Bear with a smile, as she glances at her wrist-watch. "We're in pretty good time," she murmurs. "The doors aren't open yet." Moving quickly round towards the front of the store, Mrs. Bear and Rupert fall in behind a long queue of ladies. Rupert tries to peep past them. "We're an awful long way from the entrance to the store," he says. "Are all these people going in? Why don't they move on?" More ladies arrive behind them, and at length there is a buzz of talk and they start forward. "See," says Mrs. Bear, pointing to a hat in the window. "There's the chief thing I want to buy here." And Rupert looks carefully at it before they move on again.

RUPERT LOSES SIGHT OF MUMMY

The crowd sweeps in with such a rush,
Rupert is jostled in the crush.

He struggles from the seething throng,
But Mrs. Bear is swept along.

"Rupert! I thought that you were lost!
I must sit down, at any cost."

"I've lost my nice hat, that's the worst,
Another lady got there first."

As the crowd nears the main door they go faster, until they are swept into the great store in a flood. Rupert is pushed from side to side and squashed between other people. "Whew, this is weird," he puffs. "I've never seen Mummy and Mrs. Sheep and Mrs. Badger as excited as this. There must be something very important here." Struggling out of the stream, he is just in time to see Mrs. Bear forcing her way round a corner. "What a tearing hurry she's in, she isn't looking round," he mutters.

"I expect she thinks I'm still just behind her." But in a moment she is out of sight, swallowed up in the seething crowd, and he decides to wait in case the pressure eases. It is as well he does so, for after some time the worried face of Mrs. Bear appears again. "Oh, Rupert, I thought I'd lost you," she exclaims. "Look, here's a quiet spot. Let me sit down. Oh dear, I'm tired out. And I'm feeling so *annoyed*!" "Why, has something gone wrong?" asks Rupert.

RUPERT CAN'T CARRY MUCH MORE

"Should we get parted, don't despair,
Just catch the bus home, here's your fare!"

"This staircase goes up all the time,"
Laughs Rupert, "there's no need to climb!"

Mummy buys blouses, gloves and such,
Soon he is holding far too much.

"I can't keep up!" He makes a note
Of Mummy's gaily patterned coat.

Mrs. Bear tries not to cry. "It's that nice hat I wanted so badly!" she says, nearly sobbing. "Somebody else got there first and I just missed it. Never mind. We must press on. There are other things I want. And in case we lose each other again here's some money so that you can catch the bus back to Nutwood without me." And she starts off towards the upper floors. "My, this is a jolly staircase!" laughs Rupert. "We're going up although we're standing still." After leaving the moving staircase Mrs. Bear buys several things, and gives Rupert two parcels to hold as well as some smaller packages to go in the carrier. Then she takes him to join in the scramble at the glove counter, and pops another packet into the carrier. As she moves away as briskly as ever Rupert becomes anxious. "I can't carry much more through this crowd," he thinks, "but I must keep Mummy in sight. Thank goodness the pattern of her coat is easy to spot."

RUPERT DROPS SOME PARCELS

Then someone gives his arm a bump,
He drops one parcel with a thump.

After his parcel Rupert crawls,
Just then a small red object falls.

"What's that?" The red thing disappears,
Beneath the counter Rupert peers.

Not finding it, he gazes round,
Now Mummy's nowhere to be found!

The reason for Rupert's anxiety is soon very clear. Trying to follow his Mummy through so many shoppers is no easy task, especially at the rate she is going now. Various people bump into him before he can get away from the glove department, and he drops one of his parcels. Stooping to pick it up he drops the other, which rolls away, and he has to grope to collect everything. While he is on the floor a small reddish object falls from somewhere, and out of the corner of his eye he sees it bounce away. Rupert is not sure whether he has seen anything fall or not. "There's just room for a little thing to go under this counter," he murmurs. "I can't see. It's all dark. Anyway, nobody seems to have lost anything, so perhaps I was wrong. I mustn't waste any time." Getting up, he finds the crowd is less dense for the moment, and he gazes round. "Mummy's not in sight now," he sighs. "Which way did she go? Oh dear, I really don't much like this kind of shopping."

RUPERT FINDS HE IS MISTAKEN

Between the shoppers Rupert goes,
Then spies a pattern that he knows.

He keeps that coat within his grasp
But at the door, he gives a gasp.

"You're not my Mummy! What a shame!"
Cries Rupert. "But your coat's the same!"

"I'm sorry!" Running in again,
He waits and watches, all in vain.

While he is hesitating Rupert has a bright idea. "Mummy brought me up that moving staircase," he thinks. "If she's going back to the main entrance she'll have to go back down the other one. If I can go down first I may see her on the way out." So he is soon on the ground floor continuing his search. To his delight, after a long wait he catches a glimpse of the familiar pattern on a coat moving as fast as ever, and he dashes between many people to keep close to it. Rupert has to work hard to keep up. "Whew, Mummy's going faster than ever!" he puffs. "She's not normally so excited." At the door he gives a gasp for the owner of the coat looks round. "Hello, it's a little bear," she says. "Do you want me?" "Oo, I'm s-sorry!" gasps Rupert. "I thought you were my Mummy. You've got the same sort of coat. Oh, dear, I must go back." And, while the smiling lady goes out, he returns to find a quiet spot from which he can see as many people as possible.

RUPERT WANTS TO EXPLAIN

A manager, so tall and smart,
Asks, "Missed your Mummy? Don't lose heart!"

"Little lost persons need not fear,
We have an office for them here."

A smiling nurse says, "Never mind,
All this will turn out well, you'll find."

"You'd better tell me who are you,
What's your address? Have you come far?"

For some time Rupert stands waiting as a lot of people stream past him, and at length one of the shop managers comes up to him. "Well, little bear, you look worried," he says. "Is anything the matter?" "Yes, I've lost my Mummy," says Rupert, "in this terrible crowd." "Ah, you'd better come with me," says the man, leading Rupert into a passage where a notice points to an office for lost children. "But I needn't go there," declares Rupert. "*I'm* not lost. I'm here! It's my *Mummy* who's lost!" The shop manager seems amused at Rupert's words and does not stop until they enter an office with two or three doors and are confronted by a smiling motherly nurse. "Well, well, and is this a little lost person?" she says kindly. "Dear, dear, never mind. Shall we put our parcels down and take off our overcoat? It's warm in here. Now shall we jot down some notes on who you are? Rupert Bear of Nutwood, eh? Well, don't be frightened."

RUPERT HEARS EVERY WORD

Says Rupert, "There's no need to fuss!
I've got some money for the bus."

"We'll give your name out, little bear,
On our loudspeak— oh, who is there?"

As Rupert peeps out, with the nurse,
A voice complains, "I've lost my purse!"

"It's only small, a reddish shade,
But there's lots in it, I'm afraid."

Rupert is still worried as he jumps down from the chair. "You needn't tell me not to be frightened," he says. "I'm *not* frightened, but my Mummy will be. I'd better take the bus home. She gave me some money." Then the shop manager comes back. "Now then, have we got his name?" he asks. "We'll put a message over the loudspeaker system." But at that moment there is the sound of an agitated voice beyond one of the doors and the man goes to find out who is there. While Rupert and the nurse wait in the office there is more loud and urgent talk outside. Something he hears makes the little bear move towards the door. He cannot help hearing every word. A lady in a fur coat is complaining that she has lost a valuable purse. "It was only a little one," she says. "A dull reddish colour, but it had a lot in it. I can't imagine where I dropped it. Or did I leave it on a counter? Or, oh dear, are there pickpockets?" Rupert has slipped into the corridor and gradually creeps nearer.

RUPERT INSISTS HE CAN HELP

The little bear decides to speak,
"I think I've seen the purse you seek!"

"I saw a little red thing drop
And bounce off, somewhere in the shop."

The man exclaims, "Near Gloves, you say?
We'd better look there, straight away."

"Oh dear," thinks Rupert, "this is grim,
I'd better keep tight hold of him!"

The lady talks so fast that the shopman cannot get a word in until Rupert screws up his courage to interrupt. "Go away, go away, little bear," says the man. "I'll see you in a minute. This matter is more important. Yes, Madam, pray proceed." But Rupert won't be silenced. "I really think I can help," he insists. "I was shopping with my Mummy when I dropped my parcels and something dropped near me and disappeared. Something reddish in colour. Oh my, if I could remember just where in the shop it was." The shopman and the lady stare at Rupert and hesitate. Suddenly the little bear gives a start. "I think I remember now," he exclaims. "My Mummy was buying some gloves just where I dropped my parcels." "Ah, Glove Bargains!" says the man. "That's easy to find." And asking the lady to wait in the office, he hustles Rupert down yet another wide passage and back into the store. "Whew, I must keep tight hold of his hand," thinks Rupert.

RUPERT PEEPS BELOW A COUNTER

" I think that this may be the place,
It may have rolled into that space."

Beside the counter Rupert kneels,
Along the space beneath he feels.

" The very purse! It's past belief!"
The man exclaims, in great relief.

" That's it!" The lady laughs with joy,
"Now, I shall buy you some nice toy!"

After working through crowds dense as ever the shopman leads the little bear into a much quieter part. "Now then, where did you drop your parcels?" he asks. "Oh, it can't have been here," declares Rupert. "It was crowded with ladies, all pushing." "Ah, but there's nothing for them to push for now," says the man, "Look, all the gloves are sold and the assistants have gone." "Then let's find a counter with a space below it," says Rupert. "Yes, this may be the one." The space under the counter is very dark and only big enough for Rupert to put his hand and wrist in as he edges his way along. All at once his hand touches something, he hooks it out with the side of his thumb, and next moment he is standing and smiling triumphantly with a little reddish object held out towards the shopman. "Well, would you believe it!" cries the man. "It's the very purse. It must be!" And, hurrying back to the office through the crowd, he shows it to the lady.

RUPERT TELLS WHAT HAPPENED

"Could I take Mummy *a surprise?*
She'd like a new hat!" Rupert cries.

"A hat like this, with flowers on!
The one she came to buy had gone."

"You've been most helpful," says the man,
"Wait there, I think I have a plan."

He calls the lady, with a smile,
Then leaves the office for a while.

The lady takes the missing purse and quickly checks what is inside. "Everything's there!" she declares. "What an observant little person you are. I owe you a lot and I should like to give you a present." "I don't want anything," says Rupert, "unless – unless I could take Mummy a present. She wanted a hat, but someone else bought it just as she got there." And he tries to describe the hat that he saw in the window. When Rupert has finished the lady smiles at him. "I don't think I could give you that sort of present," she says gently. "Especially if the hat has been sold." But the shopman looks thoughtful and, calling her to the side of the office, talks quietly. Meanwhile Rupert puts on his coat. "I'm glad you helped that lady," says the nurse. "She's a good customer and although she's very rich she enjoys coming to the sales just like everybody else." "Does everybody like sales?" asks Rupert in astonishment. "This one was more like a battle!"

RUPERT IS SHOWN ANOTHER HAT

The man returns. "See what I've found!"
He gives the lady something round.

Cries Rupert, "It's the very hat!
Oh, how did you get hold of that?"

"It's from our new stock, quite the best,
Not in the Bargains, like the rest."

Then taking Rupert to the door,
The lady leads him from the store.

Rupert is ready to go. "I've been here too long," he says. "Mummy is sure to have left the store by now." However, the lady bids him wait a few minutes. Soon the shopman, who has been out, re-enters the office and again they talk in quiet voices. Then the lady sits down. "Now then, little bear," she says, "is this anything like the hat your Mummy wanted?" "Why, it's exactly the same!" he cries. "It *is* the hat. I thought Mummy said someone else had bought it. How *did* you get it?"

The shopman grins at Rupert's excitement. "This isn't really the hat your Mummy saw," he laughs. "It looks like it, but this is a better one from our new stock. This kind lady has decided to buy it for you because you have done her a good turn. Won't your Mummy be surprised! She is going to get a wonderful present!" He quickly wraps paper round the hat, and before Rupert can thank her properly the lady takes it and another of his parcels and leads him out of the store.

RUPERT RETURNS IN A BIG CAR

"A bus to Nutwood? There's no need,
My car will take you there, at speed."

A splendid car waits in the road,
And Rupert steps in with his load.

At Nutwood, he arrives in state,
A few yards from his cottage gate!

"My, you've been quick about your tasks!
But where is Mummy?" Daddy asks.

Outside, when they are free from the shopping crowd, Rupert takes a deep breath and thanks the lady as nicely as he can. "And now if I can have the hat and my other parcel I must catch the Nutwood bus." "Nutwood? Did you say Nutwood?" says the lady. "Yes, we live there," smiles Rupert. "Then I can get you home much sooner," the lady tells him. "Come with me." She sounds determined, and before he knows what is happening he is being shown into a big car by a very smart chauffeur. The great car travels so smoothly and fast that the journey seems very short before Rupert recognises his own village. "It's lucky that my way goes through Nutwood," says the lady. "Now out you get, and thank you again." When he is a little way off Rupert turns for a last smile. Then he scampers home and is met by Mr. Bear. "Hello, Daddy, here I am at last," he says breathlessly. "Has Mummy been very worried about me?" "She isn't back yet!" says Daddy.

RUPERT SOON GOES OUT AGAIN

Anxiously, Rupert tells him all,
Then swirling snow begins to fall.

"I'll meet the bus!" Off Rupert goes,
"Oh, good!" He spies a coat he knows!

"Rupert! You got here! I'm so glad!
Oh, what an anxious time I've had!"

"My poor feet! How they bother me!
Quick, Daddy, make a cup of tea!"

Rupert has a lot of explaining to do to make his Daddy understand why he isn't with Mrs. Bear. When he has finished Mr. Bear gives a sigh. "Well, I'm not surprised that things went wrong," he murmurs. "I've always thought that Winter Sales ought to be forbidden by law!" "Ooo, I say, look!" exclaims Rupert. "While we've been talking it's been snowing heavily. Mummy will be more anxious than ever. May I go and meet the next bus?" Daddy says he may and soon Rupert is trotting out again. As he approaches the bus-stop through the driving snow Rupert sees the big shape of the bus already there and among the people trudging away from it is his own Mummy, looking very tired and dispirited. "Oh, *Rupert!* You're here, you're safe!" she gasps. "Oh my, I must get indoors and sit down. Oh, my poor feet!" Rupert helps her to the cottage and into an arm-chair. When he has put the kettle on for tea Mr. Bear returns with an amused look in his eye.

RUPERT SURPRISES MRS. BEAR

"Three parcels! What's this extra one?"
And Mummy gets the bag undone.

"My lovely hat! It can't be true!
How did you get it? Tell me, do!"

She tries it on. "It suits me fine,
I can't believe it's really mine!"

"You battled for it, like a knight!"
Laughs Mr. Bear, in great delight.

When Mr. Bear has teased her about her outing Mrs. Bear feels better, and taking off her coat she sets about her housework. "Ah, there are your parcels, Rupert," she says. "You did well to get them all home. But, wait a second. You had only two parcels and the carrier bag. What's this other one?" "Open it and see. It's yours!" smiles Rupert. Next minute she is staring in amazement. "It's my hat!" she whispers. "It *is*, but it can't be! I saw it sold. How did you get hold of it?"

When she hears that the new hat is a present from the rich stranger, Mrs. Bear tries it on in delight. "How lucky that your eyes were sharp enough to spy that red purse when it fell!" she says. Then they all have tea. "Well, I'm glad it's over," laughs Rupert. "Next year *you* must go to the Sales, Daddy, and see if you have an adventure as good as mine." Mr. Bear pretends to shudder. "Oh, what terrible, *terrible* things you say," he grins. "I'd be *much* too scared of all those ladies!"

Follow RUPERT
every morning in the
DAILY EXPRESS

ANOTHER ISLAND PUZZLE FOR RUPERT (page 97)

Three palm trees, Nos. 13, 21 and 28, each stand due south of another palm and due west of yet another, but on the last page of the Blue Star story the old Professor says the treasure is buried on the south-west coast of the island, so palm No. 28 must be the answer.

Published by Beaverbrook Newspapers Ltd., Fleet Street, EC4A 2NJ and printed by Purnell and Sons Ltd., Paulton